Priscilla ✔ KT-173-016

CHARLIGH GREEN
vs THE
SPOTLIGHT

PUFFIN

PUFFIN BOOKS

UK | USA | Canada | Ireland | Australia
India | New Zealand | South Africa

Puffin Books is part of the Penguin Random House group of companies
whose addresses can be found at global.penguinrandomhouse.com.

www.penguin.co.uk
www.puffin.co.uk
www.ladybird.co.uk

First published 2022
001

Text copyright © Priscilla Mante, 2022
Interior illustrations by Sophia Watts
Illustrations copyright © Penguin Random House Children's, 2022

The moral right of the author and illustrator has been asserted

Set in 13/18.5pt Sabon LT Std
Typeset by Jouve (UK), Milton Keynes
Printed and bound in Great Britain by Clays Ltd, Elcograf S.p.A.

The authorized representative in the EEA is Penguin Random House Ireland,
Morrison Chambers, 32 Nassau Street, Dublin D02 YH68

A CIP catalogue record for this book is available from the British Library

ISBN: 978–0–241–48203–2

All correspondence to:
Puffin Books, Penguin Random House Children's
One Embassy Gardens, 8 Viaduct Gardens, London SW11 7BW

MIX
Paper from
responsible sources
FSC
www.fsc.org   FSC® C018179

Penguin Random House is committed to a
sustainable future for our business, our readers
and our planet. This book is made from Forest
Stewardship Council® certified paper.

PUFFIN BOOKS

CHARLIGH GREEN
GREEN
VS THE
SPOTLIGHT

Also by Priscilla Mante

Jaz Santos vs the World

In loving memory of my maternal grandmother.

To Alexandra, I hope you're shining
bright up there.

Prologue

Good evening, ladies, gentlemen and – most importantly – cats. You're all very welcome to Charligh's World. My name's Charligh – which may not or may not be spelled Charli on my birth certificate, but I think you'll all agree that the 'gh' gives it a bit more PIZZAZZ. And, darling, there's nothing that a girl like me, who was born for the stage, loves more than pizzazz, apart from big hats, tabby cats and hitting the high notes.

So, what else do my fans want to know about me? Well, I'm left-handed, red-haired, and I do my best to bring vintage and retro glam to

Bramrock. I play defence for Bramrock Stars FC, the world's best seven-a-side girls' football team. Last year we became Almost Famous after winning the first-ever Bramrock Girls' seven-a-side football tournament. I don't mean to brag, but this is just the beginning – it's likely that my upcoming lead role in the Year 6 production will be just the boost I need to achieve the next step up from Almost Famousness, which, I believe, is Super Star Celebrity status!

That is how you spell it, isn't it? *Ce-le-bri-ty*. It's certainly not the easiest phrase to say, but then the most fantabulous ones often are a bit tricky. You've probably noticed that I sometimes go off topic and dip into things that are a little irrelevant ... Don't you love the sound of that word? The way it rolls off the tongue? *Ir-re-le-vant* ...

Now where was I? Fame, yes, fame ... Well, not that long ago, I bagged the lead role in the school play *Anne and Friends*. I assumed it would be a breeze. *Spoiler alert* – it didn't go quite how I thought it would, but that's the thing with the most EPIC journeys. You might find yourself on the scenic route to your destination, but on the way you discover gems you weren't even looking for. Also ... BEWARE! There are twists and turns, detours and dead ends, false starts and grand beginnings. And don't forget the obstacles randomly planted literally EVERYWHERE that will make you fall flat on your face. Believe me, this is hugely inconvenient when your dream is to stand elegant and poised on a stage.

I must add (in case any theatre critics are reading this) that whatever I lack in the staying-up-on-two-feet ability I MORE than make up for with my undeniable stage presence, pitch-perfect singing and my very convincing accents. So there. (Also, please, PLEASE give me a five-star review.)

Anyway, without further ado, let's draw back the curtain because the Charligh Show must go on ...

Pssst! One more thing – if I hear 'bravo' and thunderous clapping at the very end when I leave the stage, I might come back out ...

1

A New Season

I placed the headphones over my ears and nodded in time to the opening beats of an acoustic cover of 'The Climb' by Hannah Montana, before launching into the first verse. I closed my eyes and eased into the flow, overpowering the singer's voice on the YouTube video. I HAD to add this to my ever-growing 'favourites' playlist – it was *sooo* good! I'd just started belting out the familiar chorus when I felt a tap on my shoulder. I jumped, and my eyes flew open to see Rhiannon O'Shea, our team coach, standing over me. Her hair was newly dyed purple – our team colour.

'Sorry to interrupt the Charligh Gorley Show,' said Rhiannon with a smile, 'but we've already started our warm-up.' She pointed over to where Jaz Santos-Campbell, my best friend and team captain, was leading the Bramrock Stars in some stretches.

'It's fine,' I said, stuffing my phone and headphones into my sports bag. 'But, by the way, it's the *Charligh* Green *Show*,' I said a bit huffily. 'Green is my stage name.'

I suppose you're wondering why I'm a tad irritated at Rhiannon and moving at a snail's pace to join the pre-game warm-up? Well, I'm not one to make a fuss, so my lips are sealed . . .

OK, OK, since you DRAGGED it out of me . . . Well, I'd arrived at the common, starry-eyed, and bursting with hopes and sparkling dreams of making my mark during our pre-season game. But I was feeling somewhat deflated because Rhiannon had made me remove the following fabulous accessories:

1. An apple-green fedora hat.
2. Giant clip-on butterfly earrings.
3. A cream feather boa.

What can I say? Clearly, I was bringing much-needed PIZZAZZ to the game. I'd been banking on her having a finer appreciation of the importance of GLAM. Although perhaps I did go over the top with the feather boa ... but it *was* January, and the temperature had plummeted to Arctic levels!

I made my way back over to the warm-up session with Rhiannon and slotted in between Layla Hussani and Allie Norton, the only two Year 5s in our team, and joined in the leg-swing exercise. It was all going well until I accidentally kicked Allie as we changed legs, because I'd moved too close to her when we turned.

'Ow!' cried Allie.

I pulled a face. 'Sorry!'

Thankfully, it was now time to move on to a five-minute jog round the perimeter of the pitch, with Steph Richardson powering ahead of the rest of the team behind Rhiannon. Jaz and Allie were next; they weren't as fast, but they're super competitive when it comes to football.

I can be competitive as well about certain things. A talent show? A singing contest? A Hollywood casting? Yes, yes and YES – sign me up, sweetie! However, some things are just not worth throwing my hat in the ring for, and running is one of them. So I trudged along at the back, until finally we all gathered by the bag drop for the pre-game talk.

'Is everyone ready to beat the Havencroft Doves?' said Jaz with a grin.

When we're off the pitch, Jaz and I are always incredibly busy making each other laugh, but on the pitch everything's different. Her focus is razor-sharp, and once the whistle blows she takes NO prisoners!

'*Yesss!* I can't wait for our first game of the year!' said Layla.

'I hope we haven't lost our touch,' said Talia Janowicz worriedly.

You know those optimistic people who always expect the best, see unicorns EVERYWHERE, and look for the silver lining? Well, Talia is NOT one of them.

Layla is, though. 'Don't worry, we haven't!'

Layla's dark hair was in the highest ponytail ever, and she was bouncing on her tiptoes like a fuelled-up rocketship ready for take-off. Right now, I was slightly jealous she had this much energy after the gruelling, soul-destroying, so-called 'warm-up' jog. And no, I'm certainly NOT exaggerating! I'm exceedingly fortunate to even be standing here to tell the tale (if doubled over, clasping your stomach, is classed as 'standing').

'Layla's right – we've got this! I'm so ready for the match,' Allie said confidently, pulling on her goalkeeper gloves.

I straightened up, finally catching my breath again. 'I hope the Doves are ready . . . to lose, that is!'

Rhiannon signalled two minutes to the Doves' coach, who was walking her team on to the pitch. 'OK, it's five-a-side today. This is just a friendly to warm us up for the seven-a-side league, which starts next week, but let's give our first match of the year our very best! Every game's a chance to refine our skills and put into action what we learn in practice.

'As you know, this new league brings the opportunity to be seen by scouts to train alongside the Women's Super League in their two-week residential Summer Soccer School, which is like a pre-academy foundational skills programme. Since we're playing in fives today, obviously two of you will need to sit out. Sadly, one of them will have to be you, Steph, because I know it's still one more week until you get the final sign-off from the doctor to play . . .'

Steph smiled heroically. 'My sprain has healed really well; at my last check-up yesterday, there was no pain or tenderness. It must be all the fruit, veg and rest I had over Christmas.'

We all cheered loudly, especially Naomie Osei, who is Steph's Very Best Friend. Naomie, Steph, Jaz and I have always been the Fabulous Four since we met back in Year 1. Things are a little different now we share our fabulousness with Talia, Layla and Allie in the Bramrock Stars FC.

'Love the enthusiasm! And the second person to sit out will *beee* . . .' Rhiannon's eyes darted round our huddle.

'Me! I could do with recuperating after THAT warm-up,' I said, sighing loudly for effect and giving Rhiannon a hard look, which seemed to be lost on her.

'Brilliant, you and Steph can wait by our bag drop. As for the rest of you, let's get into our starting positions!'

I sat down next to Steph, whose gaze was firmly fixed on the match as soon as the whistle blew. As for me, well . . . I have HEAPS of fun playing football, but watching it isn't quite the same. Being on the stage – erm, I mean pitch – is more ME. I'm just not a sit-on-the-sidelines kind of kid.

My very sincere intention of quietly sitting still was tested when, after approximately sixty seconds of not saying a word, I almost *heard* Naomie's fluorescent-green water bottle speak to me; it was practically crying out to be used as a microphone.

I could resist the call of the mic no longer. Grabbing it, I cupped it in both hands and held it to my mouth as I jumped up.

'You're tuned into Bramrock FM with Charligh Green reporting on our town's most loved football team, Bramrock Stars FC, aka the Dreamers. Seven minutes into the game and Talia Janowicz has just made an immaculate pass to

Jaz Santos. Can the team's star striker get an early goal with that killer left foot? Ouch, unlucky! The ball was saved . . . by the crossbar – lucky for the Doves because their goalie's out of her depth.' I said bravely, undeterred by the chilly looks I was getting from our opposition. I switched to a Mancunian accent as I continued with my insightful commentary.

'The Devious Doves have stolen possession again. How they managed to get the ball off the reigning champions is anyone's guess. Now they're zigzagging down the wing – sneaky, but they're not as clever as our left back Naomie, who has blocked the ball.'

I paused as a Dove took hold of the ball yet again and pelted with it down the centre, speeding round Layla and booting it into goal. Allie leaped across and – BOOM! – punched the ball away. 'Hurray! And how wonderful to see Allie punching balls and not boys today!'

Allie glared at me. She did have a short fuse sometimes, and I didn't want her to self-combust, so I decided to wrap up my sports presenting for now. I sat down and yanked my hat back on.

'Nice hat,' said Steph with a smile.

'Thanks. Mum found it for me in the Christmas sales, and I was just dying to come and show it to you all.' I tilted my fedora to one side, got my phone out, smiled and took the perfect selfie.

'Talia said Rhiannon couldn't let me wear it because it was against health-and-safety rules, but clearly she's never considered the danger posed by not looking fabulous,' I said.

Steph giggled, but really it was no joke. I had spent a LOT of time picking out the perfect hat for our first match of the year.

At least my FABTASTIC glamour would be appreciated in our school's musical adaptation of *Anne of Green Gables*. See, I'd been cast as Anne Shirley, yes, THE Anne Shirley, and in approximately twelve weeks, two days and four hours I'd be giving my first-ever OFFICIAL performance.

Not that I didn't perform all the time – I had a YouTube channel that would have had tons of viral videos if my dad didn't restrict it to a private account (*sigh* – more on that later!). I'd also sung at last month's Christmas carol concert, the Year 5 talent show, AND I make up my own songs, plays and puppet shows all the time. But

THIS was my first time acting in a proper scripted play. So I'm taking my stage career EXTREMELY seriously this year!

'How cool is it that scouts are coming to watch us play later in the season?' Steph said. 'Jaz is the very best in the Bramrock Stars – she has to get a place in their Summer Soccer School! And get this, our team get funding for each player who goes on to be selected for an academy in September if they complete the Summer Soccer School. That would help a lot – we're always running low on funds.'

Steph is team secretary, and it suits her because she's super organized and responsible. Naomie helps her with our club accounts because she's the class maths genius.

'We've so much going on this year – SATs, Summer Soccer School scouts, the new league and –' Steph furrowed her brow – 'anything else?'

'The play! How could you forget the play?' I burst out.

Steph giggled. 'Just kidding, obviously. I *am* the stage manager, and you *do* remind us quite a lot. Seriously, though, you're going to be amazing! Don't forget us when you're famous.'

I blinked. 'And you are . . .?'

We both exploded with laughter.

Of course, when I become famous, I'll NEVER forget my best friends. I plan to have it all – fame, fortune *and* friendship!

2

On the Road to Stardom

After half-time, Naomie was subbed for me, and finally it was my turn to shine. I was playing right back, and Allie said my job was to keep the ball from going anywhere near her. A tall girl pelted down the wing, and I managed to block her, kicking the ball back against her calves so it bounced off the pitch, leading to a throw-in. I flung my arms up in victory and faced the sideline, smiling at an imaginary crowd as I waited for the referee to pass the ball back to me for the throw-in.

I threw it, but the Dove marking Layla slipped in front of her. Luckily, it was a good throw so it went sailing over her head – and Layla's – right into Talia's path. She pushed the ball up about twenty yards, outrunning the Dove who was marking her, before blasting it into the net. YES! Our second goal – it was 2–1 to the Dreamers now.

There were just a few minutes to go, and I moved up to give Jaz backup after she won a tackle from the Doves' right back. Just as I was running up, a Dove regained possession of the ball and charged down the centre. I went in for a tackle. This was my moment – or least it should have been – but somehow my feet became tangled and I fell with a BUMP on my bottom.

There were two ways this could go. Either I could stand up, dust myself off and look exceedingly silly or . . .

'Aaaaaaargh!' I yelled, grabbing my knee. I scrunched my face up and blew shaky breaths in and out for added effect.

EVERYONE was convinced. Rhiannon blew the whistle to pause the game, and the Doves and Dreamers crowded round me. My heart swelled with pride – my acting skills really were THAT good!

'Everyone give Charligh some space. I do hope we haven't got another injury,' Rhiannon murmured, crouching down next to me.

'Don't worry, Rhi, we haven't.' I leaped to my feet and gave the audience my bounciest star jump as I waited expectantly for resounding applause.

But can you believe it? I didn't get a SINGLE clap. *Tough crowd*, I thought as they began to disperse.

'You're not allowed to do that,' said Talia, folding her arms. 'You can actually get carded for faking like that.'

'Well, I just did, and it's acting not faking,' I said indignantly.

Rhiannon grinned. 'Talia's right – I'm only smiling because I'm so relieved you're not hurt. But you shouldn't do that! Ever heard of the boy who cried wolf?' she said, raising her eyebrows.

'I've been watching the men's World Cup football highlights at Jaz's house, and they were jumping and diving all over the place!'

I didn't get what all the fuss was about. I mean, I'd shown myself to be LITERALLY World Cup material!

'Well . . .' Rhiannon said. She stopped, apparently lost for words. 'Well,' she started again, 'this is the girls' grassroots game – we don't do that here!'

She turned back to the others, who were now waiting impatiently. 'Sorry about that interruption. Last three minutes, girls. Let's go!' She blew the whistle to resume play.

I did manage to rein in my stellar acting skills for the rest of the game, and the final score was 3–1 to us! While I won't give myself all the glory, I did play a massive part in setting up Talia's goal, and (more importantly) my World-Cup-worthy performance gave the game the sparkle it needed.

After the game, I got into the back of the limo (driven by my chauffeur) with my manager and my two bodyguards on either side. Why was I calling the chauffeur 'Mum'? Well, since you seem to be a stickler for detail, it's because technically it WAS actually my mum at the wheel, and yes, it was my dad next to her, and we were driving to our house on Orbit Drive. You must admit that it's *infinitely* more fun to pretend I'm a rich and famous actor who gets chauffeured around.

I'll have all that one day. However, at this moment in time, the two people on either side of me were actually my two-year-old twin brothers, Rory and Reuben. Unfortunately, right now, they were screaming, snorting and laughing – a true cacophony of horror. Mum says they're just going through the 'terrible twos'. They *are* the terrible two, in my opinion, but she calls them her 'miracle babies'. Mum didn't think she could have another child after me, and then she did – and not just one, but two at the same time.

'So!' I shouted over the din of my little brothers. 'The season starts in two weeks. We have a game scheduled nearly every weekend until the first week of May and then . . .'

'Erm, Charligh?'

'Yes, Mum?'

'We'd love to hear all about football later, but right now can you please entertain your brothers so the roof of this car doesn't fly off with the noise?' Mum said.

I nodded. I was clearly the most entertaining Gorley, so this was definitely a job for me! I began by drowning the Tinies out with a rendition of 'Born in a Manger' from *Nativity*.

'Noise over more noise,' Dad said.

How. *Rude*.

Fancy comparing that dreadful din to my dulcet tones! I stopped abruptly mid-chorus and glared at the back of Dad's grey-flecked hair. 'Fine, shall I just stop then?'

Mum elbowed him when she pulled up at the lights. He still didn't say anything, so she called out, 'You're doing great, Charligh. We love festive songs.'

'In the middle of January,' Dad muttered.

But he piped down as Rory and Reuben – who had fallen silent – looked at me with wonder. At least the Tinies knew star quality when they saw it, but I couldn't really blame Dad for struggling to recognize my unique talents. See, the thing is – and there's no polite way of saying this – he's the B-word. It's rather rude, so I'll spell it out: my dad is B-O-R-I-N-G. *Maybe* he was fun before he became OLD (it was his forty-seventh birthday last year!), but nowadays he's a real snooze-fest. It's no surprise, considering his work involves another B-word, which doesn't bear mentioning. Spell it out again? OK, it's B-O-O-K-S.

He's the Director of Information Resources at Bramrock Academy library. And yup, it's INCREDIBLY weird that a girl like me, queen of PIZZAZZ and GLAMOUR, is the daughter of someone obsessed with books and 'literature'. Dad says I wouldn't be here if it wasn't for books because he and Mum met in the university library where he used to work, when Mum was doing research for one of her archaeological digs.

My mum was a qualified archaeologist, and she *could* have become *the* female Indiana Jones, but now she's a teacher (massively less cool), and she spends a lot of time reading history books and marking history homework. She works at Bramrock Academy too, teaching GCSE history.

I can tell exactly what you're thinking. How unlucky can one girl be? But, except for their stale-grey jobs and their adoration of books, I love them the most in the entire universe – though PLEASE don't tell them I said that. You can mention the stale-grey bit, just not the love-them-so-much thingy, because Mum would get all weepy – I know she would.

'Do you need help with your maths homework, Charligh?' Mum asked.

'No, I'm on top of it,' I said confidently. *On top of it* meaning I'd given up completely because I just don't have a maths kind of brain.

'Hmm . . .' Mum said, not sounding very convinced.

Thankfully, her attention turned to something else, as there were workers drilling ahead, and part of the road was closed. Dad groaned – he does that a lot – but Mum just made a gentle U-turn and went round the other way, down Crescent Avenue. Both Naomie and Steph live on this street, so I waved at their houses as we went past, even though they couldn't see me. The Tinies started waving too. It's super cute, but it's also a bit annoying how they copy everything I do – especially Reuben. At least they never copied my face – so I still have that.

I have thick red hair, a huge sprinkle of freckles on my face and cerulean blue eyes, which is basically a dreamy way of saying deep blue. I've also got a tiny gap between my two front teeth, and I don't think I look like any other Gorley! The twins, on the other hand, have fine dark hair like Dad's, warm brown eyes like Mum's, and right now they just have baby teeth, but there's no gap so far. They might not look like me, but being identical twins they look exactly like each other. The main difference between them is that Rory is way louder and chattier than Reuben, who has yet to say his first word.

Dad's a bit anxious about Reuben, but Mum says every child develops at their own pace and she's confident Reuben will speak one day soon. I tell them there's nothing to worry about because Dad said I didn't learn to speak until the day before my second birthday and I've never really stopped talking since. Personally, I'm more worried by Rory's endless chatter – what if he grows up to be a chat-show host and outshines his extremely talented older sister? Although, at the moment, it seems the pair of them are already doing that without even trying.

'They're carbon copies!' roared Tony, the butcher on the High Street, the other week. When I was littler, before the twins arrived, he used to wash his hands, come out round the front and do magic tricks for me. Now ALL his attention goes on the Tinies.

Mum and Dad spend heaps of time fussing over the babies, OOHing and AAHing when they do things like using a potty – hurrah! If we're at the supermarket or something, and we run into my parents' friends, or even a nosy stranger, these people will go completely GOO-GAA over the Tinies and say *how wonderful it is to have twins.*

Huh ... it's like when the twins were born I became INVISIBLE to some people. I feel a bit guilty thinking like this because I do love them – they're my favourite Tinies in the whole world. They give the best cuddles, kiss my cheek every night at bedtime, *and* they make a GREAT audience for my puppet shows. Plus, being a twin is probably not all it's cracked up to be. I made a list of the pros and cons. I make lists a lot – it helps things become a lot clearer in my head. Lists of three work especially well!

So, for the THIS-TWIN-THING-IS-AMAZING side, I had:

1. Having an instant and live-in bestie.
2. I heard twins can read each other's minds and sense how the other one feels – having someone who understands you before you even say a word is pretty cool. I sometimes think that even when I *have* said a word – many words – people still don't really get me!
3. Instantly grabbing the attention of everyone, everywhere if you're just a baby who mainly babbles, dribbles and giggles.

But on the THIS-TWIN-THING-IS-NOT-SO-AMAZING side:

1. Having to share everything with your sibling, including your birthday.
2. Adults dressing you the same before you're old enough to form the words to object.
3. People calling you by your twin's name. (Now this might be fun if you want to fool people, but it could be annoying that people you know constantly get your

name wrong. Plus, your twin might do something shameful, like wear an unflattering outfit, and YOU'D get the blame for it!)

So, now that I've weighed up the pros and cons, I'm totally FINE with not being a twin and not even a BIT jealous of Rory and Reuben and their twin telepathy. At least, when I'm rich and famous, there'll be no chance of the pesky paparazzi mistaking a less talented, badly dressed twin for me, because that would be an utter tragedy. Protecting your image is very important when you have a glittering future in the public eye.

3

Centre of the Orbit

When my parents got out of the car, they each put their backpacks on and took a baby in their arms. I squeezed awkwardly past Reuben's car seat and struck a camera-ready pose on the drive, as Nancy-from-across-the-road's curtains were twitching already. I waved, and the curtains closed firmly.

I wasn't quite sure about Nancy-from-across-the-road. She isn't exactly like me – you know, a people person. Incidentally, she's also my ex-vocal coach. My singing lessons ended last spring after I delivered a spectacular rendition of 'Defying

Gravity' from *Wicked* during our lesson. I suspect she envied my ability to nail those high notes because the next day she called Mum to say she wasn't available for any more lessons until further notice. That, of course, had ZILCH to do with my opinion of her.

The main thing I missed about Nancy-from-across-the-road's lessons was her old cat, who I call Tabitha, although her real name is Gerry. Dad said I should probably call her Gerry since that's what Nancy has named her, but I think the name Tabitha suits her more. She's a plump, friendly tabby with ginger stripes and quiet purrs.

Last summer Orbit Drive had a street party, and Mrs-Mahmood-from-two-doors-down set up the mic system in her garage and invited me to sing. I sang along to tunes from *Grease* and *Hairspray*. Everyone except Nancy-from-across-the-road cheered at the end and said it was marvellous. I overheard her later ask Mrs Mahmood to keep the mic off because, 'A little bit of Charligh is like a pleasant breeze – but too much and it turns into a bit of a hurricane.'

True, I am a force of nature, so she wasn't wrong to compare me to one of life's most powerful elements. However, I had a niggling suspicion she was having a dig.

I spun round and gave a deep bow as I saw a light behind Nancy's thick curtains switch off.

'Charligh, I have no idea what you're doing, but can you please bring Reuben's car seat in? I need to give it a good clean,' Dad called from the front door.

I sighed but did as he asked. Lugging my brother's sticky, crumb-filled seat wasn't quite as glamorous as doing a mock photoshoot, but I did give Nancy-from-across-the-road a final wave as I closed the door behind me.

I pressed the button on my remote control, and my phone began to record.

'Welcome back to the *Charligh Green Show* where I talk about all things vintage and share the latest from Charligh's World! I'll start by answering a few of the avalanche of questions I received after my last video, entitled "I got my dream role".'

I left a pause for the audience-cheer sound effect I'd insert later during editing.

I held up my tablet and swiped to the notes, where I'd typed up a list of questions that I'd imagined my made-up fans would want to ask.

'Anthony, aged nine, from Swansea, wants to know how I feel about my upcoming star role, and if I'm the right person for the job.' I cleared my throat as I put the tablet down. 'I'm absolutely thrilled to have this opportunity to shine. I'm a born performer, and this is my chance to be in the spotlight.'

Great answer, Charligh Green, I thought as I gave myself an out-of-shot thumbs up. I hadn't prepared answers so I was in full improv mode now.

I picked up the tablet again and scrolled down until I found a question I felt like answering.

'Good question, Tamara, aged eleven, from Coventry, who wants to know how prepared I am for my next appearance on the stage.'

I flashed a smile at the camera. 'Extremely prepared! I previously played a significant role in my primary-school nativity . . . which didn't go as planned, but I've grown massively since then. However, you could say that this foray on to the stage as Anne Shirley is a career-shaping moment – one that will play a PIVOTAL role on my journey to fame and fortune,' I said in a hushed tone, rather pleased I'd managed to stick in 'pivotal' – the word Dad had used to beat me in our last game of Scrabble.

'I have time for one more question,' I said. 'Noella, aged eleven, from Glasgow, asks: "What's your skin-care regime?"'

'GALLONS of water, a lot of sleep and natural face masks. I'm telling you, my skin feels simply FLAWLESS after a mashed banana and honey mask!' I preened.

I heard thumping footsteps leading up to my room. 'So that brings us to the end of this brief Q and A. I hope you've enjoyed it. Stay tuned for the next episode of the *Charligh Green Show*, where everything is glamour, glitter and pizzazz!' I hit stop on my remote control just as I was interrupted by a sharp knock on my door.

'Come in,' I said testily. 'I hope your knocking isn't audible on my video.'

Dad looked at me blankly as he came in.

'I was filming,' I said, gesturing to my ring light, which glowed round my phone.

He frowned. 'Didn't you say you'd start on those maths worksheets before dinner?'

Uh-oh.

'Plan's changed . . . I'll do them tomorrow,' I added quickly, seeing Dad's frown deepen.

I had to keep Dad onside to make sure he didn't confiscate my film-making equipment – which was basically my new phone and the ring light that I'd got for Christmas. Dad had said no way was I getting a YouTube channel, but Mum said it was the sort of thing I'd be doing after the summer in high school for class projects. So, as a compromise, I was allowed to create my channel, the *Charligh Green Show*, as long as it remained on private for now.

It wasn't quite the same, seeing as the only audience I had were my parents, a couple of their friends' kids, a few of my cousins who live in New Zealand and, of course, the Fabulous Four. But it was better than nothing, and it WAS good practice for when I am famous.

After dinner, I helped Dad clear the table and put away the leftovers. Mum had made a roast, and the chicken was perfect: soft and tender, just the way I like it. If it was too squishy or dry, it would get stuck in my throat or sit weirdly in my stomach. Dad called me a fussy eater, but Mum said I just had a Refined Taste Palette, which sounded rather grand. Dad HUMPHed at that and asked just how I managed to eat all the doughnuts from Sandy's Sweet Rings doughnut stall at the Bramrock weekend market if my palette was so refined.

He was completely wrong about that, *of course*. First of all, no one had bought me ALL the doughnuts from Sandy's Sweet Rings, despite it being fairly high up on my birthday wish list for two years in a row, so how would he know if I could eat all of them or not? Secondly, I normally just stick to my three favourites from Sandy's:

1. raspberry ripple
2. iced vanilla
3. milk chocolate glaze.

Anyway, this whole clearing-up malarkey was NOT going very smoothly.

'Charligh!' Dad yelped as the glass I was carrying on top of a tower of plates shook perilously. My hands were full so I could only watch in suspense as Dad reached across the breakfast island to save it. He grabbed the glass just as it toppled off.

'Good save, Dad!' I said, impressed. My dad does not like playing team sports, but after seeing that, I think he missed his calling as a goalie.

'You shouldn't carry so much – you're just asking to drop things. I've lost count of all the plates and glasses you've smashed.'

'I was only trying to help, Dad,' I said huffily.

His tone softened. 'That was really thoughtful of you, Charligh. I'm going to put the twins to bed while your mum gets on with her marking. Why don't you find a movie to watch, and I'll finish loading the dishwasher?'

'Are you sure, Dad?' I said, feeling slightly put out, even if I was being let off housework. I hadn't smashed *that* many plates, had I?

'Definitely,' he said firmly.

I stuck my hand in the bowl of popcorn Dad had made and watched the familiar opening scene of *Lost and Found in the Big Apple*. I knew the words to every song and could recite a lot of the actors' lines from memory since I'd watched it so many times. I loved imitating the accents, body language and facial expressions of vintage actors.

Modern movies just aren't the same. Back then, it was all melodrama and fabulous quiffs. Daphne Dabello, a BIG-time 1950s actress, is my fave. *Lost and Found in the Big Apple* was one of her last films, and it was based on the real-life story of her rise to fame. The main character, Daisy Kendrick, swaps an ordinary life in a small Midwestern town for the bright lights of NYC, where she becomes a big hit, performing onstage on Broadway. Everything changes when someone from her past turns up, threatening to expose a secret and destroy her image. The actors all speak in transatlantic accents, which is like a cross between American and British.

Mum used to watch old films all the time a few years ago when she was on maternity leave and would get tired because her stomach was huge and heavy, and the twins kicked a lot. She'd make popcorn for us and put her feet up on a stool, and I'd snuggle up to her on the sofa. Sometimes she'd fall asleep before the film finished, but it still felt nice, just us two for a couple of hours after school. Now we've usually got cartoons for Rory and Reuben or the news on for my parents. Mum doesn't have much time for movies with me because, when she's not planning history lessons, she's busy with the Tinies.

I do still like watching them alone, though. I get so engrossed in the actors' performances, it's like I'm pulled into their world . . .

Speaking of performances – I couldn't wait until Wednesday. My first proper rehearsal was going to be absolutely incredible!

Daphne Dabello had three golden rules of acting:

1. Always come in with a bang.
2. Fake it till you make it.
3. You're only as unforgettable as your last performance.

The stars, the rockets . . . EVERYTHING would be going off when I made my big bang!

4

Making an Entrance

The cast of *Anne Shirley and Friends* gathered on seats arranged in a circle in the assembly hall for our very first rehearsal. The final production would be held in the Bramrock Performance Hub – a real, actual theatre! – but our rehearsals were during lunchtimes and after school. Steph was going to be stage manager, Naomie was playing the saxophone for two of the songs, and Talia was the narrator. Unfortunately, there were also two VIPs taking part in the play. Did I ever tell you about them? We call them the Very

Irritating People and I'll introduce them in order of awfulness.

First up is Erica Waters, playing the part of A Wet Blanket – just kidding, but she really could play that role FABULOUSLY. She was actually helping with set design and props, so luckily she wasn't going to be around much. Then there is Rosie Calderwood, the Queen VIP, who thankfully was too busy with ballet practice to be in the play this time – PHEW! Then the third and last part of Bramrock's Tyrannical Trio is Summer Singh, who was playing the role of Diana Barry, Anne's best friend.

Good thing it's only a play because, in real life, NO WAY could I be her bestie. Not after the way she treated me back in Reception class when the Very Terrible Thing happened. There is SO much more I could tell you about them, but let's just say that if the Bramrock Stars are the Dream Team, the VIPs are the MEAN Team.

Olly Fitzpatrick and Theo Masanga were playing the two main male parts: Gilbert Blythe and Matthew Cuthbert. They are the best of a bad bunch, which is the Year 6 boys. Olly is in the (far inferior) boys' football team at school, the Bramrock Rovers, but he is OK. I was just glad no one really awful, like Zach Bacon, the captain of the Rovers, had signed up for the play.

Mr Dodson is a new teaching assistant this term, and he was leading the production. Mrs Forrest, who is the acting headteacher (she's not, in fact, an actor but a real teacher who is taking over the role of head while the headteacher, Mrs Rivers, is off sick), said Mr Dodson would be helping in Years 5 and 6 now she was taking fewer classes. This was the first time I'd seen him up close; he had a thin moustache, a small, neat beard, and he was wearing a burgundy tweed suit and round tortoiseshell glasses. His style was impeccable!

'Welcome to the first practice. I'm so pleased to see this cast handpicked by Miss Williams. I co-wrote the script with her, and I've also added the songs throughout, which are a mixture of pieces I composed myself and old tunes that I wrote new words for to fit this production. Please call me Dodson, which is what I'm known as on the amateur-dramatics circuit.'

Summer's arm shot up. 'Your first name is Dodson, so you're called Dodson Dodson?' she said in her usual slightly mocking tone.

'I didn't say my first name was Dodson. I just said, "Call me Dodson." Listening is so essential. If you must know, I use it to separate my real life from the stage.'

Well, Dodson had come in with a bang! I knew I'd get along with him if he put the VIPs in their place more often.

I raised my hand. 'My name's Charligh. You can call me Charligh Green, sir.'

'Why would I call you by your full name?'

Quiet titters rippled through the cast, mainly from Summer.

'Green isn't my last name, it's my stage name,' I explained.

'I can call you Charligh or I can call you Green; take your pick,' Dodson said briskly.

'Charligh's fine,' I said, feeling a little silly now.

'Thank you. So, anyway . . . I hope you've all had a chance to read through the script by now – what do you think of it?'

I waved my hand in the air again.

'I absolutely loved it. Especially since it's derived from a literary masterpiece,' I said solemnly. I was sure I'd heard Dad describe books using that sort of language.

Dodson leaned his head back, his hands tucked thoughtfully under his chin. 'OK . . .'

'Charligh,' I said helpfully, although I was a bit annoyed as I'd just told him my name two seconds ago.

He looked at his clipboard. 'I'm just double-checking to see what part you're playing . . . Aha, Anne Shirley,' he said, reading down the list. 'So, tell me why you liked it.'

Well, I didn't mean I'd actually *read* the play . . . I just assumed the play would be fabulous. I stared down at the script, trying to grasp something from the first page that I could comment on, but the harder I stared, the more my brain went fuzzy, and the words turned to squiggly lines.

He looked at me, then EVERYONE else did . . . Usually, I LIKED being the centre of attention, but NOT when I couldn't actually think of what to say.

I was saved by Steph. 'I think what Charligh means is that Anne Shirley is such a fun character; she's full of passion and hope for her new life with the Cuthberts. She has good intentions, but makes a lot of mistakes.'

Dodson nodded approvingly. 'Great answer. I can see our stage management is in good hands. Good managers look after everyone,' he said. 'And this play is, of course, inspired by the well-loved classic *Anne of Green Gables* by L. M. Montgomery, but while it's similar in many ways this musical adaptation also tells its own story. We've enjoyed putting our own spin on it and I hope you all will too in the way you understand and interpret your characters and act out each scene. I think it's very important to remember that actors aren't just reciting lines or remembering stage directions, but are part of creating and telling a story.'

Suddenly another (very annoying) voice piped up. 'I think casting me as Diana was the perfect choice. I mean, Diana's the beautiful one, while her best friend, Anne, is the plain one,' Summer said, looking me up and down.

HOLD the phone! STOP the bus! WAIT *just* one minute!

SURELY it's the main character who's supposed to be the cutest one? I was stunned. This is why I prefer movies to books – they make SO much more sense. Ugh!

Although ... I suppose Summer is rather beautiful, IF you ignore her YUCKY personality. She has the straightest, shiniest long black hair and wide, light brown eyes. I think her parents made a huge mistake, though: her name should be Winter, not Summer. She rarely smiles, unless the other VIPs say something nasty, and an invisible barrier surrounds her like an ice window from which she watches everyone without actually bothering to talk to them. Not that I would ever want to get close to Summer. Not after the Very Terrible Thing.

Now that I've mentioned the Very Terrible Thing a few times, I suppose I might as well spill ...

And remember, this goes no further than us – what I'm trusting you with is highly CONFIDENTIAL, SENSITIVE information. Well, when I was in Reception class at Cross Grove Infants, we put on a nativity play. Summer was Mary, and I was the donkey. No, being the donkey is not the Very Terrible Thing. The Very Terrible Thing is that I got a slight case of stage fright. I'd been fine before we went on, but in the middle of the play I started feeling hot inside my donkey costume, and I wet myself. When I looked down, there was a small puddle of yellow at my feet. Then my face also became wet with tears.

Now, that was unfortunate and deeply regrettable, as the donkey was NOT supposed to pee on stage, or cry. That wasn't Summer's fault at all, but what happened next was. You see, the ice queen and I used to be best friends. In fact, she was my only friend! Believe it or not, back in Reception class I wasn't the very cool social butterfly you see now – I was more of a shy, awkward caterpillar who didn't fit in. And, after that moment in the nativity, everything changed. Summer treated me as if I was no one – I just stopped existing to her for the rest of the school term.

Luckily, my mum was just starting her new job so she decided I should go to a school closer to her, and she managed to get me into Bramrock Primary Reception class after the Christmas holidays. So it became quite easy to avoid Summer. But then, to my absolute horror, when I started in Year 1, she came over from Cross Grove Infants too.

She's never spoken to me about what happened, but every once in a while she'll fix me with this LOOK – and I just know she's quietly mocking me. That's why Daphne Dabello's 'fake it till you make it' motto makes a lot of sense. NEVER let people like Summer know when they get under your skin . . . or when they hurt you (not that I was hurt by her, of course!).

Ever since my humble beginnings as a donkey, I'd been waiting for this moment in the spotlight, and no one, especially not Summer, was about to dull my shine! So I gave her my best I-Could-Not-Care-Less look and shrugged my shoulders.

'How lovely. Does Diana have no personality too?' I asked.

Summer scowled. 'I guess it's lucky for some that Miss Williams was in charge of the casting, and there were no actual auditions,' she shot back.

I flushed hotly. How dare she suggest I was picked because Miss Williams likes me, rather than for my obvious outstanding flair for drama?! But, just as I was about to retort, Dodson cut in.

'There was no nepotism involved in this decision. I wasn't part of the process, but I've heard that Charligh performed amazingly at the Christmas carol concert at Bramrock Shopping Centre, and she's always the first one to volunteer to perform skits.'

'Um, what's nepotism?' asked Olly.

'It essentially means favouritism.'

Dodson raised a warning eyebrow in both mine and Summer's direction before turning back to the rest of the class as I was still simmering.

'We will, of course, be happy to confirm that everyone has the right role and maybe do a bit of reshuffling, but I don't think that will be necessary. So, is there anything anyone likes, or doesn't like, about the characters?'

'I like how my character, Matthew Cuthbert, is so kind and, even though he doesn't fully understand her, he seems to really take to Anne the moment she arrives on Prince Edward Island,' Theo said.

'Where?' I whispered to Steph.

Canada, she mouthed back.

Personally, I was more of a New York City or LA kinda gal, but Canada would have to do, although I hadn't really practised my accent for that. Speaking of practice . . . I put my hand up once more.

'Mr Dods– I mean, Dodson – when will we start actually rehearsing?'

Naomie nudged me. I opened my eyes wide at her and mouthed, *What?*

OK, perhaps that was a bit blunter than it had sounded in my head, but . . . we *had* been here for a full fifteen minutes and hadn't even got started.

'This is rehearsing, actually – actors must immerse themselves in the world in which the story takes place, and not only know their character, but understand the other characters too. So I think this is a perfect time for us to play the superpower ice-breaker. I'd like you all to remain in this circle and go around, introducing which character you're playing, and telling us if you could pick one superpower what it would be. Let's start with Anne,' Dodson said.

I stood up, glad of the chance to stretch my legs. 'I'm Anne Shirley and my superpower would be . . . hmm . . . let's see . . .' I paused, enthralled by all the possibilities whirring about in my mind. 'Like Dorothy, from *The Wizard of Oz*!'

I burst out triumphantly. 'You know, when she clicked her heels and could go back to Kansas? Well, I'd click my heels and be able to go anywhere in the world. You know, Paris, Milan, Beijing, New York, all the places where the fabulous, fashionable and famous people hang out and I'd –'

'OK, thanks for starting us off,' said Dodson briskly, interrupting me again. 'We'll go anti-clockwise, so let's hear from Steph next.'

I sighed deeply. My thirty seconds under the spotlight had been and gone for this rehearsal. The show-stopping ride that was playing the lead was taking a while to get going, but it'd be worth it in the end when all eyes were on me under the spotlight ... and no one would EVER forget my performance.

5

Team Tactics

I trapped the ball with my right foot and passed to Steph, who'd moved closer to the goal. I ran down the centre, and Steph curled it into the goalkeeper's box. As it flew towards me, I could see the Formsby Phoenix goalie moving out wide towards the left corner. I was close enough to get a touch on the ball first, so I stepped forward, turned my back and gave it a firm shove into the centre, and in it went. Hurray! My surprise goal took us to 4–0 just after half-time – and it was my very first goal!

'*Perfeito!*' shouted Jaz. 'We're flying! Even our defence is scoring now.'

Steph high-fived me. 'Well done, Charligh!'

'Go, Dream Team!' shouted Karina and her sister Katy, who were next to Rhiannon and Miss Williams on the sideline. Karina and Katy were two-thirds of the K triplets from Year 5, some of our most vocal and loyal fans. Miss Williams lets them come along in our minibus sometimes for away games if there's extra space.

I gave them a grand bow before running back to the other end. I was still high on the absolute thrill of scoring my first goal when I got there. 'Isn't this exciting, Layla!' I shouted across the pitch.

She frowned, shook her head vigorously and pointed. I was confused for a second until I looked to my left and saw the number 4 Phoenix midfielder had blasted the ball down into our half and slipped past Steph and Naomie. I ran up towards her, but she confidently dribbled the ball wide of me, and once she got past I knew there was no chance of me overtaking her.

'Defence!' yelled Talia.

I was already out of breath from earlier, and the slow pace I was running at wasn't gaining any ground with number 4. Before I knew it, she'd kicked the ball into the net, skimming it over Allie's head. And just like that the Phoenixes had bounced back.

Over the next ten minutes, our opponents managed to slap two more goals in the net, narrowing our four-goal difference to only one. We spent a tense final minute scrabbling about, defending wildly, determined that no more goals would be conceded. There was a collective sigh of relief when the whistle blew – we had only *just* managed to hold on to that win.

After the match was over, and the minibus had dropped the K sisters home, it took us to the library, where we gathered in one of the meeting rooms Rhiannon had booked for us to talk about our strategy for the year ahead. Rhiannon and Jaz were standing on either side of the whiteboards, pens poised.

I tried my best to stifle a yawn. To be honest with you, I would have been happy missing this part. But I knew – because Jaz told me ALL THE

TIME – that our team meetings were just as important as the games.

'How did you all feel about your first match of the season? You're off to a winning start!' Miss Williams said.

'Yes, but things went downhill after my FIRST goal,' I said. 'Our lead narrowed after that first goal I scored.'

'Can you say "my first goal" again?' Allie said sarcastically.

'How many goals have you scored then?' I shot back, hands on hips.

'OK, that's enough, girls,' Miss Williams said. 'I think I'll start by saying that, overall, we played well, and of course we got the result we wanted. Let's look at what we can do to improve.'

'Miss Williams is right. A win is always a good start to the season,' Rhiannon said. She scribbled TEAM TACTICS in blue pen on the whiteboard. 'Who wants to start?'

'We go out and annihilate our opponents by winning every single game, because we're the Dreamers!' I pumped my fist in the air only to be met with blank faces.

'That's not a strategy,' said Talia flatly.

I sighed. *There she goes again: Talia with her grey-sky thinking.*

'Really?' I said. 'Winning seems like a pretty good strategy to me, unless you have a better one.'

'Talia's right,' said Rhiannon gently. 'Aiming to win every game's great, but in this context strategy is more like a long-term game plan. The new league brings fresh opportunities, more chances for us to grow. What's our overarching vision, and what tactics are we going to use to get there?'

'We've always done the two-two-two formation, but I think we need to be open to trying something different,' Jaz said.

'Well, it's worked well for us so far, so why change?' I asked curiously.

'Our current formation might not work with every team, though,' said Talia, frowning.

'Right. Sometimes it depends on the strengths and weaknesses of our opponents and also their formation. We won't always know much about them, but we should find out as much intel as we can,' Jaz said.

'Like who their top scorer is,' added Naomie.

54

'Or what position they are in the league,' said Layla.

'Perfect. All great ideas. Write that up, Jaz,' Miss Williams said.

'We can make our game stronger by using our strengths to compensate for our weaknesses. We're good at pushing the ball forward and putting pressure on our opponents' defence, but when the other team does manage to break through our defence, sometimes we lose our cool a bit.'

'I agree – as soon as the defence slips, it's like an avalanche. The rest of us are forced to fall back and play defensively, which takes us away from our ultimate goal of scoring,' Naomie said.

'I had to save four shots in a row today,' Allie said with a scowl.

'You're the team goalie,' I said. 'Aren't you *meant* to save things?'

'Yes, but the defenders are supposed to keep the pressure off,' Allie snapped.

'It's not just about defence, though. We need to make sure the forwards don't let the ball get so far down the pitch in the first place,' said Layla.

'Good point, Layla,' said Jaz, looking thoughtful.

'Hang on. What about building up our fan base?' I said.

Talia blinked at me slowly. 'Our *what*?'

'Our fan base,' I repeated, amazed that no one else had thought of it. 'It's nice Katy and Karina come along, and that our parents attend some matches too, but we need more fans.'

'I don't think that's really part of the strategy we're talking about right now,' Layla said.

Talia nodded. 'We're going to give our best performance every week, but not because we want to get more popular.'

Speak for yourself, I thought. What was the point of giving our best performance with no audience?

I shrugged. I'd tried, but now I'd exhausted all my good ideas, so I didn't say much for the rest of the meeting as the others made suggestions about team tactics. None as good as my idea, if you ask me. We also had a look at the fixtures table for the season, a grid that displayed the team name and match date and also two blank columns, one for the match result and another for info. Jaz said it was for when we knew more

56

about each team and what position they were in the league.

At the end of a very long hour, our team planning session was over, and it was time for Rhiannon to start her shift at the library.

Miss Williams beamed at us. 'Just before you all go, I'm happy to tell you that the PTA has agreed to fund the cost of a football residential course during half-term. That means you and the Bramrock Rovers will be heading to the New Forest for five nights, where you'll receive training from football coaches and choose from a range of fun activities in the afternoon.'

She pulled out a pile of letters from her brown leather bag and passed them round.

'Your parents just need to sign these and pay twenty pounds towards the coach fare.'

'This is SO good, miss – football training every day!' Jaz exclaimed.

'I've been to the New Forest,' said Layla. 'It's so pretty down there – the scenery's beautiful.'

'It will be like a massive long sleepover,' I said, feeling absolutely thrilled.

Since the twins were born, we hadn't gone anywhere – and this was even better than a holiday with my family because I'd have my friends to do fun stuff with. AND we were all going to come out with the best football skills and win the league. What more could we ask for? This was going to be the best trip ever.

Everyone was picked up or walked home until it was just me and Jaz left in the library. We headed to the beanbags in the children's corner to wait for her mum. I was going with her to her mum's house in Brighton for lunch, then her Aunty Bella, who her mum lives with, was driving me back to Bramrock.

Jaz's mum (who always tells me to call her Iris – so cool!) moved into Bella's a few months ago. At first, it was VERY awkward. Jaz's parents weren't even talking, and poor Jaz felt stuck in the middle! She says they're acting more like grown-ups now, so Iris comes over most evenings to see Jaz and her older brother, Jordan. At the moment, they're trying this new arrangement where Jaz and Jordan take turns staying at their mum's at weekends.

I'd said to Jaz that at least she gets her mum all to herself without her brother there, and she rolled her eyes. I suppose it doesn't feel that way to her. She's big on teamwork and everyone pulling together, which is what makes her such a good captain of the Bramrock Stars – and the BEST friend ever.

'Rather you than me, kid,' I drawled, looking at the old battered copy of *Anne of Green Gables* that Jaz had plucked from one of the bookshelves. I plopped down on a beanbag before promptly rolling off it, my legs sticking up in the air. *Gah!*

'Oh, Charligh! My Aunty Bella does this thing at her gym called Pilates. She says it improves your balance. Maybe you should consider it,' Jaz said, giggling.

I snorted with laughter as I moved to a plastic seat. 'That's a NO to Pilates *and* to reading *Anne of Green Gables*. I've got a script. I don't need to plough through the whole book.'

Jaz rolled her eyes, so I went on. 'I understand you love books, but you know how I feel about them. The characters just aren't the same as the ones onstage or on a screen. They're flat, like the pages they're written on, they lack PIZZAZZ, and some of the details just don't make sense.'

'You could always flash it at Mr Dodson to make it look as if you've read it,' Jaz said, grinning.

'Now *that's* an idea!' I took the book from my best friend's outstretched hand. 'Image IS everything, as Daphne Dabello says.'

6

Back in the Spotlight

My bedroom has pale lemony walls that make it look like it's always sunny, even on a gloomy winter's afternoon like today. I have tiny butterfly-shaped fairy lights that hang high up on my walls. I think butterflies are the prettiest things ever, and when my room is dark, and they're switched on, they light it up with different colours. My carpet is blue, and I like the stillness of that colour. It makes me feel calm, which was particularly helpful at that moment because, after two hours of hunching over the script at my desk, I was in SERIOUS danger of feeling less than calm.

Why weren't these lines sticking in my head? My eyes swam as they tried to drink in all the words I had to learn, and it felt like each time I blinked I lost my place.

OK ... I had to learn this script. I decided to break it down and put an asterisk next to all of Anne Shirley's lines. I didn't need to learn everyone else's part, did I? Just my own.

This is much easier, I thought, feeling pleased I'd figured out a short cut.

So this time I ran through it, skipping the dialogue belonging to everyone except Anne, and I managed to read to the very end of Act 2. This script was *way* longer than I'd thought. Well, Rome wasn't built in a day, was it? I jumped up and did a short series of my bounciest star jumps in an effort to wake myself up. The good news is it actually worked, and I perked right up.

While doing my jumps, I remembered that Dad had been moaning about the mess in my bedroom. So, with my newfound burst of energy, I decided to pick up and organize the sea of clothes on my floor. This was less due to a sudden love of tidiness and more fuelled by Dad's latest threat not to buy me anything more from Golden Age (Bramrock's best vintage store) until I organized the clothes I already had and started keeping my room neater. And that just wouldn't do! You see, I had my eye on a magnificent bottle-green coat in the window that I NEEDED to get Dad onside with buying.

I ended up putting on 'When Will My Life Begin?' from *Tangled* and making a bit of a song and dance of it as I sorted and organized my clothes, books and all the STUFF that was basically lying everywhere in my bedroom.

Time goes past so fast when you're pretending to be a Disney princess, wondering when your life will begin. So before I knew it, it was nearly 8 p.m., which was an hour from my bedtime. I had two options. I could:

1. start to learn lines again, or
2. record a new video for my YouTube channel.

I chewed my lip, thinking hard. I did have to learn my lines, but surely I could sneak in some time in front of the camera where I could say something about our upcoming football residential course? I started with the recording, and it went well, except I sort of lost track of time, pretending the Dreamers had a legion of fans waiting to hear our latest news. It was 8:50 by the time I'd finished, but ... I'd nailed it!

There wasn't much point squeezing in ten minutes' practice, was there? Football training, the team strategy session and tidying my room must have really tired me out. I yawned as I got ready for bed. There was always tomorrow, right? Although I did have to finish off that geography project and get my maths homework done ... I'd start learning my lines after that, I thought as I dozed off.

On Tuesday morning I hummed along to my big opening song, 'Here Comes Anne', as I unpinned my hair from its rollers, and it sprang up in big bouncy red curls. I checked my reflection for the last time in the hall mirror. One thing was for sure: Summer definitely wasn't going to outperform me.

Here's what I planned to do . . . I was going to roll up to that stage, ooze star quality and deliver my lines FLAWLESSLY, and, well, Dodson would be literally bowled over by my talent! Sure, I hadn't actually read through the whole script, and yes, I didn't know half the lines even in Act 1, let alone the other two acts, but I knew I'd DAZZLE everyone up there today with my PIZZAZZ and talent.

'Before we dive into the script, I thought it'd be fun to do an ice-breaker to get us thinking about enunciation, pace and expressing emotions,' Dodson said. 'I'll give you a tongue-twister: *red leather, yellow leather*. Repeat after me . . .'

'*Red leather, yellow leather, red leather, yellow leather*,' we chorused.

We repeated this a few more times, and then Dodson pressed his thumb and index finger together, making the OK symbol, then he pulled a jumbo soft ten-sided dice out of his plastic box.

'This is my feelings dice. On each side, there's a single word conveying an emotion or mood. Depending on which emotion you get when you roll the dice, you'll say "*red leather, yellow leather*" in that way, and the rest of us have to guess the emotion.'

Amazing! Here was a chance to show Dodson exactly just how expressive I was.

The first person to go was Neeta. '*Red leather, yellow leather*,' she said slowly, squinting and looking round sharply as she said it as if observing her surroundings.

Naomie guessed correctly – the mood was *suspicious*.

Theo went next. His one was *happy*, which is funny since that's kind of his permanent mood. When it got to me, I flicked my wrist, throwing the dice up so it spun quite high, then dropped right through the space in between my body and outstretched hands. Not the catch I was hoping for, but as I looked to see what the dice had landed on it read *petrified*. I took a deep, shuddering breath and breathed out in a high, wobbly voice, '*Red leather, yellow leather*,' as I clenched my fists and drew my shoulders up to my ears.

'Scared!' shouted Sebastian.

'Almost,' I said.

'Terrified?' Steph suggested.

'Petrified,' said Summer.

'Isn't that just the same as scared?' asked Olly.

'Not exactly,' Dodson explained. 'Petrified and scared are synonyms, but there can be a slight nuance, which is a difference in meaning. It's those so-called little details that can really make your performance stand out the way it should. Great work, everyone – I could almost feel your emotions, and that's the job of an actor. To make the audience feel.

'Now could you all please take out your scripts, and can everyone who appears in the first two scenes assemble in the centre here. As for the rest –' he opened his arms – 'spread out. No need to be sardines in a tin when we have all this space. By show night, we need to have got used to projecting to an audience of hundreds, who'll be filling a much bigger space than this. And we'll do some vocal warm-ups for a few minutes while our opening actors have another look over their lines and position themselves.'

I budged up next to Talia, and Theo, who was playing Matthew Cuthbert, and Neeta, who was playing Marilla Cuthbert, came and joined us. We all spent the next few minutes hunched over our lines, silently reading, until Talia said it was time for us to arrange ourselves for the opening scene.

It felt weird shuffling around in the space marked out for us on the floor. I was so used to being higher up, on the stage. Everything just looked different down here. Finally, we were all in our opening positions while Talia stood to one side and read the introductory narration.

After Talia's bit, it was time for the opening song. The cast began with the chorus:

'Here comes Anne,
The girl with the dreams, the hope and the
    fears.
Anne the quiet, Anne the loud.'

Then it was my turn to break in with the opening solo verse.

'Imagine if there was a kingdom sparkling
    beneath the Lake of Shining Waters.
Would I fit in a world that is far away from
    what I'm used to?
Imagine there's a city nestled inside the trees.

I wonder if the stars know how beautifully
    they shine.'

I launched into the rest of the verse, imagining how this was going to sound when I was up onstage in front of an audience. I wasn't normally nervous, but knowing Dodson was sitting there was making me feel self-conscious, so my voice shook a little bit as I held the last line, but only for a split second.

'Bravo! A round of applause for Charligh, and Naomie on saxophone,' Dodson said, the first proper smile breaking out on our drama teacher's face.

'That was amazing,' Steph said. She made the heart sign with her hands on her chest.

'You've got us in the mood of the play, that's for sure! And that's what singing is all about – transporting us to another world. I can just see Anne now at the train station with her suitcase, full of dreams and aspirations,' said Dodson.

A burst of colour sparked and sizzled inside me.
Bang! Crackle! Whizz!

Finally, I'd made my entrance! Now for the first scene. I took deep breaths in the one-minute break Dodson gave us, replaying the words over and over until I saw him giving us the thumbs up. Time to continue.

Anne walks on and stares into the distance, a hopeful smile flickering on her lips.

Anne: I wonder what they'll be like.
          I wonder what it will feel like.
          To be part of a family.

She gasps, clutching her small, thin fingers to her heart, and looks left.

'Charligh! You're looking the wrong way,' I heard Steph whisper from the side.

I frowned. I was SURE it said left. Then I realized I was walking right. I was all wrong, and Steph was right, as usual.

'Carry on,' called out Dodson. I knew he meant to reassure me, but it made me feel a bit flustered.

Matthew Cuthbert wanders on to the stage with a shy smile, and, holding his hat, he squints at Anne.

Theo ambled on to the stage.

Matthew: Are you the boy, erm . . . the
            child from the orphanage?

*Anne skips towards Matthew and clutches his
hands.*

Anne: I am so thrilled! I do believe this
            is the best moment in my life, and
            I will cherish it forever. You are a
            kind man, Matthew Cuthbert. I
            know I've just met you, and I
            know it's silly to judge people
            you've just met, because if anyone
            was to look at me . . . Well, there's
            not much to look at, but anyway
            the point is I can just tell, with
            you, what a kind man you are.

My hands were clasped under my chin, and I
stared at Theo. And then I kept staring . . .

I was stuck, and my gaze had frozen on
his slightly bewildered-looking face while I
rummaged around in my brain for the next lines.

I knew that Anne launches into a full monologue here . . . but why couldn't I remember the words? I'd just read them a few moments ago before rehearsal started, but now the lines were slipping away, mixed up and stuck together just like a plate of spaghetti. I looked down at the script again. Drat, I'd lost my place. Now this was embarrassing. I mouthed the words to the previous scene, following along with my finger until I got to the right place.

I tried again, but the words just escaped my head. I bit my lip.

Amarachi whispered the first line to me after Dodson gestured to her.

| Anne: | It has taken a great deal of self-restraint for me not to collapse and cry with utter happiness and relief. |

I repeated it quickly, then I squeezed my eyes shut and opened them again, reading the next bit while Theo said his line. I was trying, desperately, to dredge the rest of the monologue up from my memory.

It was my turn again. I opened my eyes again, then my mouth ... but nothing came out, not even a trickle. There was a terrible silence in which I could almost hear Summer gloating, even though I couldn't see her.

Dodson's face was a closed book as ever, but I knew exactly what he was thinking, and I felt a burning shame when he asked me to take out my script and read from it. No one else had to do that.

Each time I lowered the script and looked away and attempted it one more time, the words – each and every last one – would betray me and march out of my brain. Even the lines I did read straight from the stupid script sounded weird and stilted, or I stumbled over the words. So much for being a natural. By the end of the rehearsal, I had a splitting headache, and my brain felt like scrambled eggs! It was ALL going wrong.

7

Flora House

Well, so far, it didn't feel like playing Anne was going to be the top-notch performance that would propel me to international fame, not unless I wanted to go viral in an internet video captioned 'DISASTROUS PERFORMANCE RUINS SCHOOL PLAY' – definitely not the kind of publicity I was looking for.

The bell signalling the end of lunch break rang, and everyone rushed out of the hall to head back to class. I stayed behind, pretending I was looking for something in my bag.

I wanted Dodson to say something, that he believed I could do it, or even that he *never* believed I could do it, and I should prove him wrong, but he was staring down at his papers and scribbling little notes. Eventually, he looked up and squinted at me questioningly.

My heart and shoulders dropped. So there it was: the only thing Dodson had to say to me was a big fat NOTHING. The only thing worse than a bad impression is NO impression. A Very Terrible Thing had happened back in the Reception class nativity, and now the Very WORST Thing was happening.

The Dreamers walked behind Miss Williams and Rhiannon up the path to Flora House nursing home, which was a large salmon-coloured detached house with a path cutting through an immaculate front lawn that led to a white front door. Don't get me wrong; I'm all for charity stuff, but getting my hands dirty doing gardening for other people definitely comes LAST on the list of ways I like to spend my Saturday mornings.

This was Steph's idea. She'd seen a call-out for 'Helping Hands' volunteers at Flora House, and she hadn't stopped going on (and on!) about the importance of football teams giving back to the local community. Jaz said it's called corporate social responsibility and got hooked on the idea because she's seen professional football teams do it.

Talia did point out that, when people talked about football players giving back, they probably meant ones like Messi and Ronaldo who had millions, but I suppose it wouldn't hurt for me to practise for when I do have millions. And who knows? We might even get another spot in the *Brighton Chronicle* if a journalist caught wind of it.

You can never be too prepared for these things, so I'd come dressed to impress, just in case. I was wearing a red-and-black dress, soft brown leather ankle boots and my bottle-green duffel coat. Cleaning my room had paid off in the end. Mum had gone with me to the vintage shop in the High Street to try the coat on, and it was a perfect fit, so we bought it right there and then. I loved it!

'Hello and welcome, everyone,' said a woman who introduced herself as Nari Joon.

Nari looked about the same age as Miss Williams, and she had a buzz cut and wore feather earrings that matched her cloudy-pink polo shirt that all the staff there wore. She was the new activities and volunteer coordinator for Flora House and wanted to build up the volunteer programme.

'This is a two-storey building, and there are some residents' rooms on the first floor, but upstairs is mainly where we keep supplies. It's much easier for the residents to get around on this level.' Nari said. 'Many of our residents have mobility issues and, while we do have lifts, some persist in using the stairs. It's the only exercise that a lot of them get, especially in the winter. Although we do encourage all our residents to use the grounds for walking in, and we can provide assistance for those who need it. Now something important for you to be aware of is that some of our residents have dementia.'

'What's that?' asked Allie.

'It's actually the name used for a whole bunch of degenerative brain conditions,' said Naomie.

Nari gave an appreciative nod to our Team Encyclopedia, aka Naomie. 'That's right. I'm afraid it's not a very easy thing to live with. The impact on dementia sufferers and their loved ones can be significant. They may get lost or forget a familiar face or misplace things. Skills like reading, writing and basic maths might become a challenge. Sufferers can also struggle to follow conversations and might experience mood swings, anxiety and depression. They may also have physical symptoms, like tremors or slurred speech.'

She paused and took a breath. 'Now this may seem like a lot of information to take in, but I wanted to give you a brief overview of dementia so you understand what's going on in case any of our residents display any of the signs. This is not a one-off conversation. If you want to hear more about it, you can always pull me aside or one of the other staff members: Mina, Simon or Dami. And we'll always be around, keeping a close eye on you. We strive to ensure that everyone is happy and safe here.'

'That must be so hard for the residents,' Layla said quietly.

Everyone else looked as if they were still taking it all in. It was so quiet you could hear a pin drop. I wondered if any of the residents were even up.

'Can we get started with the volunteering?' asked Allie.

Nari smiled. 'It can be hard, Layla, and yes, Allie – you can get started! Thank you all once again for volunteering to help. I'm especially looking forward to having the Bramrock Stars working on our garden as we get a bit closer to spring, although I understand some of you want to be of assistance in other ways?'

Jaz swung her bag of books in the air like a pendulum. 'I'm going to read to some of the residents. I have a stack of books they might like, but can read any of their favourites too.'

Layla raised her hand shyly. 'I'd like to paint their nails.' She was carrying a metal box filled with an assortment of nail polish.

'Some of them would love that!' said Nari. 'Now let's go into the main communal area – you'll find a lot of the residents spend their time there.'

We wandered through and saw about fifteen older people dotted round a large lounge and kitchen area. The first thing I noticed was surely the reason why this place was called Flora House – an explosion of floral colours and designs everywhere! The eggshell-coloured walls were decorated with stencils of sunshine-yellow daffodils, red poppies and flame-coloured roses that met at points on the wall in a kaleidoscopic firework of colours. There was also a large canvas painting of a flower-filled landscape above the piano. The second thing was that it was no longer quiet. There was happy-sounding chatter and bursts of laughter in different pockets of the lounge and mini-kitchen.

While Jaz and Layla settled down with the residents inside for reading and nail-painting, the rest of us were taken to the garden by Nari. We spilled out through the patio doors into a wild and crowded back garden that contrasted with the immaculate grass patch at the front. There was a metal bench on each side of the patio doors. The rock garden in the left corner of the garden closest to us was overgrown with weeds, and a scattering of tired-looking flowers lined the whole left-hand side. The grass lawn extended to a brick back wall, and in the right-hand corner furthest away from us there was a small plot of messy soil that Nari said used to be an allotment where the residents grew vegetables like tomatoes and runner beans.

Steph wasn't joking when she'd said the garden needed a lot of work. Ugh, this was even worse than I thought. I kicked a weed that was peeking out between the paving slabs and hoped midday would come soon.

8

A New Friend

Miss Williams, Steph, Naomie and Allie, armed with garden tools and small reusable plastic trays, had begun the dull process of uprooting the weeds in between and round the rock garden.

'Good luck,' I muttered before giving the loudest sigh I could manage.

'Are you OK, Charligh? You can help us if you want,' said Steph.

'Oh, I'd love to,' I said insincerely, 'but . . .' I kicked out my right leg sorrowfully and pointed at my new boots.

'Why did you wear your smart boots to do gardening?' said Talia, who had a bucket of hot soapy water and a brush and was cleaning the path that ran round the side of the lawn. Allie tittered as if I'd done something silly.

I sighed. Neither of them are exactly fashionistas, shall we say. Talia's hair kind of sat on her like a sad mushroom because she refuses to let anyone cut it except her gran, who clearly isn't skilled in that area. And as for Allie, well, the only time she isn't wearing tracksuits is when she is in school uniform.

'Because they complement my new coat,' I explained patiently.

'How do boots give compliments?' Allie spluttered.

'No, not that kind of compliment. I mean the boots go with the new coat,' I said.

'And what a magnificent coat that is! What's the name of the young person wearing it?' came an amazing voice from behind me. It was clear and melodic, and I spun round to see an old woman with papery-white skin and a nest of silvery-blue hair that was wrapped round huge rollers. She was sitting on one of the black metal benches, wrapped in a grey-and-white woollen blanket, with a plump cushion behind her.

'Charligh,' I said.

'That's a nice name. Short for Charlotte?'

'No, just Charligh. With a "gh". My mum spelled it C-h-a-r-l-i, but it just didn't have enough PIZZAZZ for me.'

I didn't usually tell people that, because they didn't seem to get it, or even laughed at me as if I'd said something really hilarious. But the old lady nodded like she understood. She had glasses hanging from her neck on a rose-gold chain.

'Nice to meet you, Charligh. My name's Betty Langton.'

She seemed kind of cool for an old person, I supposed, and talking to her was a good way to get out of Steph's weeding mission.

I sat beside her on the bench. 'Did you dye your hair blue?'

'How did you guess it wasn't natural?' She gave an impish grin. 'How about your hair? Is it dyed?' Her eyes danced happily, and I couldn't tell if she was joking.

I grinned. 'No, it's not! I'm not sure if I'd ever do that – I love my red hair. It goes wonderfully with my freckles.'

'You have a wise head on young shoulders,' said Betty, and this time she looked serious. 'Are you a gardening enthusiast like your young friends here? Is that how you know each other?'

'Hmm, not really. I play football with the Bramrock Stars – all the girls here are my team-mates,' I replied.

'Ah, the Dreamers,' Betty said. 'I read about you in the *Brighton Chronicle*.'

'Did you?! Yes, that's us,' I said with a grin. 'We're the Dreamers, and this year our biggest goal is to win the league. But I have another, even bigger dream.' I stretched my arms out as wide as they could to emphasize just how huge it was. 'I'm playing Anne Shirley in our school play, and I want to be the best Anne EVER.'

'Well, imagine that!' Betty said. She sounded very impressed. 'You must be really talented to get the lead part, and you must love acting too. Have you ever seen any musicals or plays yourself?'

'Mum took me to see *Matilda* in the West End last May for the big one-oh. That's ticked off my list. I've also seen the *Prince of Egypt*, *Frozen* and *The Lion King*, and I'd love to see *Cats* live one day, but I already know the whole soundtrack.'

'These are all splendid shows. You have marvellous taste in plays, young Charligh. Is *The Lion King* still playing at the Lyceum? That was the one theatre I never performed at during my time in the West End.'

A thrill ran through me. 'You were on the stage?'

'I was indeed, mainly as an actor, though – I didn't have one of those really big singing voices, so a lot of the time I'd be in the chorus, but when it came to non-musical theatre . . . now that was my forte. Then, after I stopped acting, I became a visiting teacher at various drama schools all over the world.'

'That's *my* dream,' I gasped. 'I'd LOVE to do what you did – travel round the world with a theatre company, sparkle under the spotlight and meet my fans. Then maybe, when I'm a little older, I'd like to be a Hollywood star or do some TV presenting . . . if I have the time.'

'Well, as long as you're willing to work for it, I have no doubt you'll get there.' Betty chuckled. 'I hear the passion and determination in your voice – it reminds me of a younger me.'

I suddenly thought of something. 'Did you ever miss your friends and family when you travelled?' The twins were annoying, but I couldn't imagine being thousands of miles from them or my parents.

Betty's face clouded over as if remembering something, and then she stood up. 'Wait here. I've got something I'd like to show you. It's upstairs, which is a no-go area for you young volunteers!'

I sat and waited – very patiently for me – and five minutes later Betty was back, clutching a large round brown box. She sat down on the bench and then paused, resting her hands round the sides of the box.

'Sorry for the wait,' she said. 'I'm not as young as I used to be, and those stairs took me longer than I thought. I learned my lesson and took the lift back down.'

'That's OK,' I said politely. 'I turned ten last year, and I take the lift instead of the stairs sometimes as well because I'm less likely to trip inside a lift.'

Betty burst into peals of laughter, which made me laugh too, even though I hadn't actually meant to be funny.

'I got this bamboo box as a gift from some very kind hosts I had on my third visit to India. Everyone said it wasn't very practical because it's round and not square like all the other boxes I had, so it would be difficult to fit in when I packed things up, or when I put my boxes in storage. But sometimes the things that stand out are the best. Anyway, it's what's inside that's important.'

Betty set the box down between us and pulled the lid off.

My eyes widened. I could see beautiful fountain pens, a brown leather bookmark with tassels – my dad would love that – and also postcards, photos and letters still in their envelopes.

'Are these the postcards from when you toured with theatre companies?'

Betty nodded, passing me a bundle of postcards. 'Yes, and photos with the actors and friends I met along the way. So, to answer your question, yes, I did sometimes miss my loved ones, but I also made new friends in the cast – we lived, ate, sang and acted together, so really we became a sort of family too.'

'That sounds a bit like the Bramrock Stars.' I looked over to where my friends were digging around in the soil. 'Although we don't all get along,' I said, thinking how snappy Talia and Allie had been with me lately.

'Do you have a friend called Betty?' I asked curiously as I turned over one of the postcards with a picture of a black sandy beach on it. It was the third postcard I'd noticed that was from and to 'Betty'.

Betty shook her head. 'No, I'm the one and only Betty in my circle, but I'd sometimes send postcards back to myself with some fleeting thoughts I'd scribbled down while at the post office.' She laughed. 'I'm not really sure why I did it, and I know some people back home were a bit confused when these postcards came through the letterbox, but it was my little gift to myself. As much as I adored being up on stage, I also loved those quiet, private moments putting my thoughts down on a postcard, or writing a letter to a dear friend, or recording the more private things in my journal.'

Betty perched her glasses on her nose, then rummaged around in the box some more. She pulled out a faded pink envelope and looked at the address on it. 'This is a letter my niece wrote to me describing her university graduation, which I sadly wasn't able to attend.'

'Did you miss a lot of things when you were away?' I asked.

'I did indeed. Acting is hard work and involves a lot of sacrifice. You'd be surprised at what people give up, and it's not to say we didn't have our celebrations, but it's no walk in the park! Sometimes you don't see the results immediately – it's like your friends over there planting seeds. The flowers don't instantly spring up, but, when it's their season, they grow bold, beautiful and strong. My advice to you is to enjoy every season!'

She slipped the letter back in its envelope and placed it in the box. 'I do miss having pen pals. Nowadays, communication is so instant, which is all very useful, but there's something rather special about letter-writing.'

Then I had my Brilliant Idea. 'Why don't we become pen pals?' I said suddenly. 'I think I'll make a good pen pal, although my Year 5 teacher, Mrs Forrest, called my writing illegible and I make a lot of mistakes with my spelling.'

Betty beamed. 'I think that's a marvellous idea, Charligh! I expect we'll be wanting your parents' permission, so I'll ask Nari to set something up since she has everyone's details.'

'My dad will love it,' I said. 'He's all about literacy being a building block of life and that kind of thing. Actually, he thinks I should spend more time working on my writing and a bit less on my YouTube videos.'

'You have a YouTube channel? Well, you really are destined for the stars,' Betty said, chuckling. 'What do you record?'

'Sometimes I do vlogs about what I've been up to lately, or showcase vintage fashion. Or I pretend to be a journalist reporting breaking news from Bramrock, and often I just sing.'

I pulled out my phone and scrolled to one of my latest videos, which showed me singing that acoustic version of 'The Climb'. I hit play before handing it over to Betty.

I chewed my lip anxiously as she listened in silence, and handed the phone back to me wordlessly. Maybe she hadn't liked it? Then my heart smiled as she stood and clapped. 'Bravo, bravo! A Bramrock Star indeed. Shine on, Charligh!'

She loved it! A real-life theatre actor liked my singing!

'Is that a new pop star you're listening to?' shouted the old man in dungarees who had been helping Allie dig.

I grinned. 'I'm not a pop star, although I am playing the lead role in my school play.'

'She's very good, isn't she, Antonio?' said Betty.

'You've got competition, Betty,' Antonio said.

'Well, she's just as loud, anyway,' said the tall woman sitting on a seat next to Talia waspishly.

'Don't worry, my wife Sylvia is like this with everyone,' whispered Antonio, giving me and Betty a great big wink.

'If you need to test out any of your school play songs on us next time, we're all ears,' Betty said.

'Or she could actually help us with the weeding,' said Talia. Sylvia nodded vigorously in agreement.

'I think my Silvia's found her twin,' said Antonio with a chuckle as he came closer.

'I think so too,' I said, giggling.

Rhiannon popped her head out of the door. 'It's time to go now. I'm so glad everyone seems to have enjoyed themselves. And well done with the gardening,' she said as Steph, Allie and Talia pulled off their gardening gloves.

'Are we seeing you next week?' said Betty as we got ready to leave.

'Definitely!' I said with no hesitation.

I didn't expect to enjoy myself so much in this house of oldies, but it had been all right. More than all right in fact – finding a new audience of people who loved my singing reminded me that I was going to do amazingly. Sure, in the last rehearsal, I'd kind of careered off the road to the stars, but clearly it had just been a tiny pothole on my journey to success. Nothing and no one was going to stop me from shining!

9

Sink or Swim

The steamy, chlorine-filled air filled my nostrils as I came out of the changing room at Waves and Wheels. I was in my favourite swimsuit, a black one-piece with white polka dots. The material was nice and smooth and silky, so it didn't make me itchy like some swimming costumes did.

Jaz, who was walking a few metres ahead, had her hair covered in a lilac swimming cap that matched her black-and-purple striped tankini. I watched her confidently climb down the stairs into the beginners' swimming pool and pull a float towards her, which she hopped up and lay backwards on.

Mum and Dad were already in the pool with the twins – I was the last one out of the changing room as usual. No matter how fast I tried to get changed, I always seemed to be the slowest to get ready. This time I thought I was being super speedy until I dropped my bag and tipped everything out on to the floor. I'd spent a full five minutes scrabbling on the ground, gathering all my belongings up, including a zillion hair grips, when Mum knocked on the door of my cubicle and said she'd see me and Jaz in the pool.

'Come on, Charligh,' said Jaz as she waved from the float. I ran in slow motion towards the pool, pretending I was a surfer about to jump in with my surfboard. But the lifeguard, a tall teenager with a skinny moustache, quickly barked, 'No diving!' from his high chair – absolutely destroying the surfer-girl movie scene I was trying to recreate AND drawing the attention of Dad!

That was the only downside of being an extremely convincing actor: people got themselves in a dreadful tizzy about things you had no intention of doing. No way was I really going to dive in. For starters, there was this teeny-tiny issue of me being unable to swim. I have to wear two orange armbands that may as well be a neon sign saying ALERT! CHARLIGH GORLEY CANNOT SWIM! I've had about a gazillion swimming lessons since I was six, and I still haven't got the hang of it. And, as if that isn't bad enough, my brothers – at age two! – already know how to swim! It was mostly just doggy-paddle, or 'baby-paddle' as Mum calls it, but at least it's something.

Look, I'm anything but a Jealous Big Sister, OF COURSE, but I couldn't help feeling they did keep getting ahead of themselves, or ahead of me anyway. Dad said I couldn't walk until I was eighteen months old, but the babies were doing it at ten months. And, although you'd never know now, I was a late starter to the talking game – but Rory said his first words just after turning one.

At least Reuben's more like me in that way, I thought.

I frowned as I watched Dad high-five the twins as they both reached him at almost the same time.

Then I made a decision. I bit my lip, sat on the edge of the pool and slid my armbands off quickly before I lost my nerve. Today was the day I would learn to swim, and what better way than plunging in the deep end?

I made my way down the ladder at the side of the pool. Suddenly I had a change of mind and wanted to go back, but a little boy was waiting impatiently to get in, with his mum standing behind him. I moved to one side, gripping hold of the ladder rail ... then something terrible happened. The babies spotted me and waved so, being the Good Big Sister that I am, I waved back with both hands, but since that meant I didn't have a spare hand ... it meant that NO HANDS were on the rail. Argh! I immediately felt myself sinking beneath the water, and I flailed helplessly for the ladder as the water rushed into my nose, eyes and ears.

'Help! I'm drowning!' I spluttered and was rewarded with a mouthful of tepid water that I choked on.

Suddenly I felt myself being pulled up by firm hands – Dad! He had reached me even before the lifeguard. He hauled me on to the side of the pool before hoisting himself out after me. I coughed up the rest of the lukewarm water as Dad patted me on the back.

'This pool water is revolting,' I said, making a gagging noise.

'It's not meant to be gulped down,' he said dryly. 'Are you OK? Where are your armbands? Did you forget to put them on?'

Thankfully, he didn't wait for an answer before spotting them and passing them over to me. OK, I'd definitely not recommend the 'sink-or-swim' approach because the reality of sinking was very real. I snuck a surreptitious look round the pool area as I slipped my armbands back on.

Jaz swam over, pulling her big float along. It had all happened so fast it seemed she'd missed everything.

'Did you see me nearly drown?' I said.

'What? No, that's awful! Are you OK?'

Good, nearly everyone was carrying on as usual. It seemed all the little kids and their parents were too busy with each other to notice me swallowing about half the pool's water. While I was truly thankful to be alive, and that I hadn't come to an inglorious end in Waves and Wheels, it made things much better knowing most people hadn't seen me Almost Drown.

'She'll be fine, Jaz. As long as she keeps her armbands on,' Dad said, giving me a suspicious look before he swam back over to Mum and the Tinies.

I stepped carefully back down into the pool and held on to the edge of Jaz's float. Just as I was thinking what a lucky escape I'd had, I saw Summer and Rosie. They must have been in the improvers' pool at the other end, and now they were making their way through the inflatable dividers to the beginners' area.

'Let's just pretend they're not here,' said Jaz, spotting them as she clambered back on to her float. 'We did call an unofficial truce.'

So last term the VIPs had accused Jaz of something she didn't do, which almost obliterated our chances of competing in the Brighton Girls' Under-11s Seven-a-Side Football Tournament. It was nearly a disaster, but they fessed up in the end to the teachers, which counts for something, *I guess*.

'Well, it looks like there will be an end to our ceasefire because Summer is just pushing my buttons,' I said.

Jaz hopped off her float. 'Here, count how long I can stay underwater for.'

I rolled my eyes. It was so obvious she was trying to distract me from the VIPs, who were now right next to us. Jaz submerged herself in the water just as Rosie shouted over, 'The fifties have called and they want their swimsuit back!'

I smiled. 'You're too kind, Rosie. That is a MASSIVE compliment – fifties is just the look I was going for.'

Luckily for me, Jaz burst out of the water, gasping and spurting out water everywhere, including in Summer's ear.

'How many seconds?' she spluttered triumphantly.

'Ew!' said Rosie as Summer furiously shook the water out of her ear. 'Why do you have to be so annoying, Jaz?'

'Who actually invited you two to stand so close to us?' Jaz retorted, quickly losing her commitment to the truce.

Summer's chestnut-coloured eyes darkened, but Rosie's mouth twisted into a smirk as she looked at me. 'It's a real shame I'm not at rehearsals to be entertained by your ... acting "skills" ... like everyone else is. But I can't wait to see the final performance. Summer has been giving me a blow-by-blow account, and it sounds hilarious. Anyway, don't worry – we're going back to the improvers' pool. You know, the one where actual swimmers are?'

'I know, I know, just ignore them,' I said to Jaz as the VIPs swam away haughtily.

'No,' Jaz said thoughtfully. 'I was actually going to say that it looks like you getting the lead role has annoyed Summer more than she's letting on. So Rosie's probably on a revenge mission on behalf of her bestie to bring you down. Anyway, can you count for me this time?' She disappeared underwater again.

Jaz was right, but not only did Summer want the main part, she thought she *deserved* it, and was telling everyone who'd listen that I wasn't good enough. She was sticking with Diana's role, just waiting for me to give up. And, if there's one thing I've learned from movies, the people you want to watch out for are the ones lurking in the shadows. Dodson had hinted that our roles weren't necessarily set in stone, and there was room for changes. Maybe my part was under more threat than I'd thought . . .

10

A Character Study

Soon rehearsals were being held twice a week, sometimes more, and usually at lunchtime. But, as we drew closer to the performance date, we started having the occasional after-school practice too.

I was still finding learning my lines really difficult. The weird thing was, a lot of the time the words would actually stick. Then, at other times, I'd sit for, like, a whole hour and go over my lines in a particular scene again and again, but this seemed to just make the words slip away more.

It wasn't all bad, though. Sometimes I'd find myself in mid-flow, feeling extremely confident and owning the stage (not to mention feeling Summer's eyes on me, ice-cold and envious), and I'd be sure I was on the road to success. But at other times it felt more like I was on a downhill express route to failure. I was certain I was saying the right lines, only to have Amarachi wave at me from the wings and then brandish her prompt cards, which actually weren't that helpful for showing me what I was supposed to say next. And whenever Dodson asked me to go over a scene again, it always led to me doing it worse than before.

By the time we got to the first week in February, I had some major things on my mind: first of all, it was one week until the half-term football residential course. And, second of all, we were less than eight weeks from our first performance of *Anne and Friends*! *Gulp*. Dodson had called for an extended rehearsal after school on the following Thursday, as it was the last rehearsal before half-term.

I was feeling nervous, but we began with a really great warm-up. Dodson started us off with some role play using cue cards – on each card, there were a few words describing a scenario and role. I had: *Badly behaved famous reality-TV star gets into trouble for letting her pet Shih Tzu poo in a restaurant.*

I really flung myself into the role, demanding to speak to the manager, valiantly defending my innocent fluffy pooch and saying that the restaurant food had made her lose control. Steph played the part of the manager, and she was brilliant too, mostly because she just played herself and was able to stay calm, defuse the situation and get the badly behaved customer (me!) to leave. I really enjoyed it, and I wished all acting could just be improvising. It'd be so much easier for people who couldn't learn their lines. And yes, OK – by 'people', I basically meant 'me'.

'Well done, everyone. That was some really great improvisation!' said Dodson. 'OK, now we're all warmed up, I'd like to approach this session a bit differently. We've run through the play as a whole, but now we're going to be doing some scene work – and really exploring what each one means and how it contributes to each character's – especially Anne's – journey. Every story holds some kind of message, and often that is communicated through the main character's transformation – also known as the character arc. So let's reflect on how our main character changes throughout the story. For all storytellers, whether you're an author, playwright, singer or actor, whatever medium you're using to tell a story, it's important to identify what you're trying to communicate to the audience and pinpoint the particularly important scenes.'

Olly put his hand up. 'What's Anne Shirley's journey then?'

'Good question!' Dodson replied. 'And just the kind of thing I want us to talk about. In Anne's case, we see a perfect example of a *positive* character arc. Can you think of any points in the story, not just for Anne, but for the supporting characters too, that are key in altering their and Anne's journeys?'

'Anne's relationship with Marilla!' Neeta called out.

'Gilbert getting cracked on the head with a slate by Anne. I think that was a big moment for everyone,' Olly said ruefully, as we all laughed.

I raised my hand. 'When Anne finally gets her puffed sleeves and doesn't have to go around in only boringly plain dresses!'

'Close, Charligh. While that does reveal a lot about Anne's personality and how much she admires nice clothes, I wouldn't say it is an instrumental moment in how her character develops because she doesn't change after it. Do you see?'

I didn't but I nodded anyway.

'I've got one,' Summer said. 'When Anne figures out there's more to poetry than stringing lots of big words together.'

'Indeed,' said Dodson, nodding vigorously. 'She learns that using simple words doesn't mean it's not poetry. And, on that note, let's move on to the scene work I mentioned earlier. Instead of going through the plot chronologically, we'll start with the scene Summer just mentioned.'

Good! One that involved me.

Olly, who was playing Gilbert, Sophia-Grace, who was playing Miss Stacy, and I positioned ourselves on the stage.

The scene began with Gilbert and Miss Stacy discussing what poetry was, and then, when Miss

Stacy turned to me and began sharing her thoughts on my work, I interrupted her, launching into my dialogue. It all came out so fast I was certain I had everyone gripped, until Amarachi began waving a sign at me that said ACT 1.

I paused slightly, turning to Amarachi, whose head was poking out from the wings. 'We're on Act Two, Scene Six, though. This is scene work, so we're not going through it chronologically,' I said, proud to have remembered Dodson's wording.

'Yes, but you're saying words from Act One,' Amarachi said.

Oops! I thought. I was reciting dialogue from another scene involving poetry from the first act. I looked at Dodson – I couldn't tell what he was thinking – then he said something to Steph, who came and handed me a script.

'Why don't you use this for now, Charligh? It's yours for as long as you need it while we're rehearsing – but I really must insist that you learn your lines by the time we get to the dress rehearsal. How does that sound?' Dodson called out.

I nodded, but I was so embarrassed. It's not like I wasn't trying, but Dodson clearly thought

I just couldn't be bothered! Needless to say, Summer looked so smug – ugh!

We went through the scene again and discussed how all the characters felt through it, but I felt a bit amateurish, despite Dodson's reassurance. A few of the cast had the script, but not any of the main characters. My voice felt suddenly smaller, thinner and more tired. Steph looked at me worriedly.

I couldn't meet Steph's eyes, and I grew tearful as I watched the next scene we were working on. It was Diana (Summer) returning home after accidentally getting drunk because of a mix-up at Anne's house.

I HATED it, especially when everyone laughed heartily, and at the end Dodson said, 'That was an extremely convincing performance.'

I scowled. The only reason Summer was getting the praise that I never seemed to attract was because she could do the one teeny-tiny thing I couldn't – memorize her lines! I knew I still had time, but it was beginning to run out. Things were NOT looking good.

11

Saturday Shoppers

'So, class, before you go to lunch, I wanted to announce a project that I think you'll find very interesting. Next term, you're going to give solo talks and presentations on a topic of your choice – although, of course, you'll need to run it by me first! Choose a topic you're passionate about and want to know more about. I'll be expecting a thoroughly researched, carefully planned and well-delivered presentation. If anyone has any concerns or questions, my office –' Miss Williams gestured at her desk with a smile – 'is always open.'

'Miss, I could do my presentation right now if you wanted me to! I already know what topic I'll choose,' I said. 'Acting! I know everything there is to know about it. Theatre, musicals, Hollywood, classic movies – you name it!'

'Everything except for learning your lines,' Rosie whispered.

I glared at her with narrowed eyes, hoping she would shrivel under my withering look. She was seriously in danger of overtaking Summer for the position of WORST VIP.

'Thank you, Charligh, but save it for next term!' Miss Williams laughed. 'You'll have a maximum of fifteen minutes – including a Q and A at the end – so you don't have endless amounts of time. Think about which *one* aspect of acting you want to cover and really dig into it. For instance, a summary of actors who have stood up for social change in the past twenty years, or maybe something that has more practical application, like tips for new actors.'

'I'd like to do my talk on acting too,' Summer said.

'Erm, no! You can't copy Charligh,' Jaz said indignantly.

'Last time I checked, Charligh didn't own acting,' Rosie said, chiming in.

Miss Williams held up her hands. 'OK, OK, girls. Let's be clear – you can have the same topic as someone else. It's not "copying", because we all bring a different perspective to the same subject and present it in our own way.'

Hmm, I still wasn't sure. Typical Summer!

The bell rang. 'And remember: the best speeches always come from the heart, so choose wisely!'

I took a long sip of apple juice and looked round the table we Dreamers share every lunchtime.

'Was it my fault for telling everyone I'd choose acting?' I said glumly.

'Don't worry about it,' said Naomie. 'You can't go back and change it, and she may have chosen acting anyway, even if you hadn't mentioned it.'

'I suppose,' I said grudgingly.

Naomie was very logical – she didn't really get the point of thinking over and over again about things that had already happened, and deep down I knew it wasn't helpful too, but I found myself doing it anyway.

'Everyone ready for the half-term football residential course?' asked Steph. Her ash-blonde hair was coiled up in a neatly braided bun today.

It looks cute, I thought approvingly.

She stabbed a fork into her battered cod. It was fish 'n' chips Friday at school, the only day I didn't take a packed lunch because I LOVED fish and chips. If I was to pick one thing to eat at dinner time for the rest of my life, that would be it (well, strictly speaking, it's two things, but you know what I mean).

'I was born ready,' I said.

I couldn't wait for next Monday. I didn't think I'd be able to sleep for the next three nights. The Bramrock Rovers, our forever-losing boys' football team, were coming along too, AND there were going to be two teams from a school in Bournemouth. I'd packed about seven dresses, a couple of my favourite costume accessories and as many shoes as I could cram into my suitcase.

'Do you think it'll be too cold to wear sandals in the lodge?' I asked.

'Sandals aren't on the checklist, so I don't think we'll be needing them,' said Talia.

I frowned. *Checklist? What checklist?*

As it turned out, everyone else had packed using a checklist that – apparently – Miss Williams had given out the other day. I felt a bit silly that I'd somehow missed it, but just played along. I'd ask Jaz about it later or dig around at the bottom of my sports bag where it was likely to be. By the sound of it, it listed really boring things like walking shoes, sports outfits and stuff like that. Yuck.

'Just make sure not to overpack! We're only allowed to bring one small suitcase and one backpack that can be used as a day bag for when we have activities,' Jaz said.

What?!

'Well, that sucks!' I said, folding my arms. I was planning to make a great impression on these new people and dazzle them with my outfits! But still, I was so excited about this adventure with my friends. And at least the checklist might give me an excuse to go shopping for anything I didn't have on it . . .

Now I loved, loved, LOVED going shopping with my mum. My dad? Not so much . . . but today I didn't have an option. Mum had a toddler playdate with the twins so Dad had 'volunteered' to take me shopping – but only after moaning that I should have showed them the checklist sooner. I knew he hated shopping about as much as I loved it, so this was sure to be a rip-roaringly thrilling experience, I thought sarcastically.

'Let's find an empty parking spot,' Dad murmured as he swerved left into the road leading to Bramrock Shopping Centre.

'Dad, everywhere will be empty,' I said. 'It's nine thirty on a Saturday morning. The shops are barely open.'

I yawned. Dad had insisted on coming here first thing since I didn't have football training this morning. The one weekend I don't have to wake up early for football practice or a game and he makes me leave the house at 9 a.m. anyway. I sighed. OK, he didn't exactly make me, but since he'd said he'd be happy to go on his own and get the stuff himself, he didn't leave me much choice. Left to his own devices, Dad would definitely come back with the UGLIEST of clothes.

'Told you,' I said to Dad, and we entered Bee & Rocks, the biggest department store in Bramrock. It was so quiet we were literally the only customers for the first ten minutes! We headed straight up the escalators to the children's section. I managed to convince Dad to buy two pairs of jeans: one midnight blue, the other a dove grey. Then I got a white top with embroidered red and yellow flowers round the edges and also a soft grey woolly jumper, AND a hooded gilet made of fake fur.

A great haul, I thought to myself.

Next stop was Bramrock Outdoor, which, as you might've guessed, is the outdoor clothes and equipment store in the shopping centre.

Dad picked up the ugliest pair of walking boots: a dull camouflage green with black trim. 'Thirty per cent discount – what a bargain!'

I took a deep breath. 'Dad, I draw the line at this. I will wear walking boots, but only if I get to choose. Those are a crime against fashion!'

Dad snickered. 'OK. I thought they were rather snazzy myself.'

I rolled my eyes. Never trust the fashion advice of anyone who says word 'snazzy' unironically.

We settled on a pair of black walking boots with striped teal-and-black laces.

I have a zillion jackets at home that were all way cuter than the ones in Bramrock Outdoor, but Dad wanted me to choose a padded one that had all these zips and pockets and was supposedly windproof, rainproof and lightweight.

'Since it's durable, you can wear it again if you ever decide to join me on one of my hikes,' he said hopefully.

I felt a bit guilty. Dad was always trying to get me to go on hikes with him round the walking trails near the Seven Sisters, but it really isn't my thing. I break out in a sweat even looking at hills – not cute!

Then we took a stroll through Bramrock High Street, and ended up at the Saturday market, where Dad and I got hot chocolate and blueberry doughnuts from Sandy's Sweet Rings.

All in all, it was a good shopping trip, considering it was with Dad and he usually spends the whole time looking like he wants to pull what's left of his hair out. He must have enjoyed it too because when we got home, and he was making lunch before Mum came back, he said we should do that again. I surprised myself by saying I actually wouldn't mind, and the truth is I wouldn't! I suppose my dad can be a LITTLE bit fun!

12

A New Adventure

It was finally the day of the football residential course! Mum and Dad made such a great big fuss when we got to the school car park. The coach was leaving at 8 a.m. sharp, but my parents being the way they are had arrived half an hour early, so it was only 7.30 a.m., and the street lights were still on.

Yes, it would be the longest and furthest I'd ever been away from my family . . . but my parents were acting as if I was going backpacking round the world or something. To me, this week spelled freedom!

After they had hugged me a zillion times, I began pulling my little wheely suitcase towards the coach while Mum sniffed and looked a bit red around the eyes. I suppose, on the plus side, it was nice for me to be the centre of attention for once and not the babies.

The Tinies burst into loud wails as I walked off so Mum and Dad fussed over them – I turned to wave goodbye again and saw that their tiny faces had gone red, redder than my hair, and their little fists were all screwed up. My eyes began to water a bit. I wiped them and tilted my chin. It must just be the chilly morning air ...

The driver was loading suitcases into the luggage compartment as other kids began boarding the coach. Mr Roundtree was standing at the side with a clipboard, ticking people off as they got on. Just then, I saw Summer cross in front of me. Ugh. She was everywhere like a bad smell! What was she even doing here? I was so busy wondering about this that – BOOM! – I walked into her, and she tutted loudly.

'Sorry,' I said through gritted teeth. 'You're not coming on the football residential, are you?' I added, fear gripping my heart.

'So you should be,' snapped Summer. 'And no, I'm just on my way to breakfast club, and I'd rather eat raw eggs than play football, but ... have fun, I guess. I was actually just going to say best of luck learning your lines on your little trip.'

'Summer, it's too early for you today. In fact, it's always too early for you. Why don't you practise smiling without baring your teeth while I'm away?' I walked away smartly before she could say anything else and joined my friends by the coach.

Layla, Steph and Naomie were standing close together, waiting for their luggage to be loaded. I saw Mrs Forrest talking to another adult, who had their back to us. Suddenly they turned, and I saw it was Dodson. Ugh! I knew why Mrs Forrest was there – she was doing her headteacher-ish duties; she'd wave us all off like she did for all school residential trips – but why was Dodson hovering around? I sighed, wondering why the universe was sending me human-shaped reminders about the lines I still hadn't learned this morning. I couldn't wait for the coach to leave so I could forget about rehearsals for a while. I was sure I'd be much better at letting the lines sink in without that pressure looming over me.

'Charligh, this is going to be so amazing!' yelled Layla, pulling me into their huddle. She looked like walking candyfloss with her rose-pink coat, matching beret and pink fluffy earmuffs.

'It would be if you girls weren't tagging along,' interjected Sebastian. He ran up the stairs with his backpack on before we could say anything back.

'Oh drat, the boys are going to get the best seats,' I said.

'No, they're not. Talia's at the front because she gets travel sick, but Jaz and Allie have already saved the back row for the rest of us,' Layla said.

'Whoop!' I cheered as we gave our suitcases to Terri, the friendly coach driver.

I plopped myself in the window seat on the left-hand side. I was sure to get the best back-seat views from there.

'Does anyone want the window seat? No? Thanks, I'll take it then,' said Allie sarcastically.

'First come, first served,' I said defiantly.

'We were actually here before you,' pointed out Jaz, taking a seat next to me. Her dark brown hair was freshly braided in cornrows, underneath a purple beanie hat.

'If you wanted it, you should have taken it. Life waits for no one,' I said sagely, settling myself into the seat.

Miss Williams switched the microphone on at the front of the bus. 'Good morning, Bramrock Rovers and Bramrock Stars! We'll take a final register in a minute, and then we'll be off, but I wanted to outline the rules and remind you of the plan for today. It's a three-hour journey to Meaden Lodge, and there is an on-coach toilet, but I'd recommend you don't use it if you're able to wait since there's often issues with the plumbing.'

She ignored the guffaws from the Rovers who were seated around the middle of the coach.

Ugh. Sooo immature.

'We'll have two rest stops, so you can go to the loo then. Also, make sure you use the paper-bag bins hanging from some of the spare seats – don't make a mess of Terri's lovely coach! Oh, and as you may have noticed, Mr Dodson has kindly stepped in at the last minute since Mr Webb had an emergency and had to pull out. And before you ask, girls, don't worry – Rhiannon will be joining us there.'

Wait . . . what . . .? Mr Dodson was coming?! OH NO! *That's why he was hanging around!*

Soon the coach was ready to go, and we were heading out of the car park. I saw all the parents waving and Mum standing next to Dad, dabbing her nose with a hanky as we pulled out. The twins were waving, and I waved frantically back. I had to make sure I kept smiling, as weirdly it felt like I might end up crying too.

My excitement had kept me awake most of the night, but now I was tired, and, once we got out of Bramrock and were speeding down the motorway, everything – from the long white stripes on the road, the gently glowing street lights, the constant murmuring from my friends and the soft purr of the coach – made me very sleepy. I tugged my blanket out of my bag and threw it over me as I felt my eyes closing . . .

An announcement blared out of the loudspeakers. 'Tonight we are very excited to have here at the

Royal Albert Hall an iconic West End star, albeit one performing in a highly interesting choice of outfit . . .'

I looked down at myself and, to my absolute horror, saw that I was wearing the Bramrock Stars strip. But there was no time to worry about that now . . . I clutched my microphone as the grand orchestra began to play and counted my intro . . . 1, 2 and 3 . . . but, when I opened my mouth to sing, nothing came out! I tried again, and out came a mixture of gravelly and high-pitched tones, accompanied by a growing crescendo of audience boos.

My eyes widened. Thousands of people sitting in the rows below were either cupping their hands round their mouth to project their disapproval or had their fingers in their ears. Eventually, my voice dried up again, and I felt myself sinking and sinking . . . Hang on, sinking? How could this be? The stage was turning to water, and I couldn't swim!

'Help! I need a life jacket,' I sputtered.

The water was rising – why was no one helping me?! A hand touched my shoulder –

*

'Charligh, Charligh! Wake up – we're here!'

I gasped and opened my eyes. Jaz was gently shaking me. She already had her jacket on, and I could see everyone else was filing down the aisle of the coach. I couldn't believe how sleepy I'd been! We'd stopped about an hour after we'd set off, to use the toilet, and I'd bought a packet of Skittles – but even they hadn't been enough to keep me awake for the rest of the journey. I'd fallen asleep and I'd completely missed the second comfort stop.

Now we all tumbled out of the coach, bleary-eyed and stiff from our long journey. I gave a big stretch as I looked around – and unfortunately poked Ricardo in the side of his head.

'Watch where you put your hands!' he grumbled.

'Watch where you put your head,' I shot back. I probably should have apologized, but I was feeling a bit grumpy after the horrid dream I'd just had.

'This is so beautiful,' breathed Layla as we took it all in.

She was right – it really was. Meaden Lodge looked a zillion times better than it did on the website. It was a very grand medieval-castle-style three-storey building made of silver-grey bricks, with turrets topped by black metal spires. It looked just the sort of place the heroine of a story might live.

I instantly cheered up, and my head began to clear. As my eyes adjusted to the midday sunshine, I took in my surroundings, all the beautiful things around me. There were birds chirping happily amid a thick border of fir trees that surrounded the large grounds, and a long straight path with logs separating us from the very green, soft and springy-looking grass, that led into a woodland area with tall, thick trees.

I wondered if this was how Anne of Green Gables felt, coming off the train and setting out in the carriage with Matthew Cuthbert? Did she hear all the songbirds, breathe in the fresh new air and wonder at the impossibly green and warm brown of the outdoors?

I sighed with happiness. It really was beautiful – maybe it would be the perfect place for me to step into Anne Shirley's shoes and finally learn my lines.

13

Explorers

Inside the lodge, things were even prettier. The high ceilings in the entrance hall had intricate plaster designs on them, and landscape paintings that almost looked like real-life photos covered the walls. The floors even had a black-and-white chessboard design!

A man with smiling eyes and a blond ponytail came to meet us. He introduced himself as Mr Kerrigan and led us into the main conference lounge that had sofas, seats and tables where we could play board games. There was even a projector for cinema nights!

'Welcome to Meaden Lodge,' Mr Kerrigan said. 'We hope you enjoy your stay and make the most of all the activities on offer. I'm not usually much of a footie fan myself, but fortunately for you we have Anders, Taheer and Elsa staying with us this spring. They are three amazing coaches from Sweden who run sports camps all over Europe.'

Mr Kerrigan walked over to one of the glossy prints on the wall. It was a huge rectangular map with tiny silver drawing pins stuck in it, which he pointed to.

'We're lucky enough to have activity instructors and even chefs from all around the world who do placements here as part of their academic studies or professional training. The history of this place is rooted in medieval England, but today it's enriched by cultures from all over the world. Each time someone comes here from a new place, we put a pin in their country to mark their contribution.'

Then he showed us all the boring important stuff like the emergency exits, the administration office ... and then, rather excitingly, started to call out the dorm-room allocations. The Dreamers and I were all in the same room – yay! Miss Williams and Dodson helped give out the room keys and a pack that had all the general information we might need in it.

Finally, Mr Kerrigan said, 'Lunch is in thirty minutes, and if the weather stays nice we can have it on the picnic tables at the back of the building, which some of you will be able to see from your rooms.'

We Dreamers decided to wait for the nearby lift up to our floor, while all the boys scrambled up to their room with Mr Roundtree and Dodson.

'Don't fancy the extra exercise, girls?' Mr Kerrigan said.

'We're just going for the intelligent option,' said Jaz.

'I like that. Now I know who the smart ones are.' Mr Kerrigan laughed as the lift door opened.

Once we were outside our dorm, Miss Williams opened the door and had a quick check of everything while we bounced around and claimed our beds.

'All right, settle down, girls! Don't forget lunch is in half an hour. And make sure you dress warmly so we can sit at the picnic tables outside,' she reminded us.

Once Miss Williams had left, we got to look round the room properly – and it seemed perfect! It had large white-framed lattice windows and thick dark brown velvet curtains.

There were eight beds in total, four sets of pine-coloured bunk beds with blue bedspreads, and a grey fleece cover folded at the bottom in case we got chilly. I threw my bag down next to one of the bottom bunks quickly because I am NOT a fan of heights, and I was completely sure I'd trip up when climbing them later, or, even worse, fall out at night if I got a top one.

There was also a large yellow sheet inside a transparent plastic folder on our door, which had our schedule:

Day w/c 17th February	Football Session*	Afternoon Activity
Monday	n/a	Boat ride
Tuesday	Football skills 1	Nature walk and orienteering
Wednesday	Football skills 2	Option A: swimming, Option B: poetry
Thursday	Football skills 3	Option A: paddleboarding, Option B: arts and crafts
Friday	Tournament	Free time/board games
Saturday 10 a.m. departure	n/a	n/a

Breakfast is served from 8 a.m.
*Football sessions run from 9.30 a.m.–12.30 p.m. daily

Hmm. I definitely wouldn't be going swimming, so it looked like it would be poetry on Wednesday for me. Which also wouldn't exactly have been my first choice . . .

'Isn't the scenery gorgeous?' said Steph from behind me. Her nose was pressed against the window.

I went to join her and stared out at the peaceful blue lake that was bordered by thick fir trees at the far end and sides.

'So beautiful. It's just like the Lake of Shining Waters!' I gasped.

'The lake of what?' Allie said with a snort.

'It's an *Anne of Green Gables* thing,' Naomie explained.

'This is a bit like Anne's adventure, isn't it? She was taken thousands of miles away from her home to start a new life on an island,' Jaz said.

'Except no one has taken us anywhere. We're only here for a holiday,' Talia said flatly.

'You have a rotten imagination,' I said.

'Come on, slowcoaches!' yelled Jaz, charging out of the room. 'Let's go and explore!'

I had had very good intentions of spending the half-hour before lunch learning my lines – just as I'd had very good intentions of learning them on the bus. But sometimes, just like in the movies, things don't always go to plan, I thought, as I skipped out of the room behind Jaz. And the lines could wait a little longer, couldn't they?

Downstairs in the canteen, I joined the queue, hoping there'd be something I liked. I could see a buffet similar to the ones we have in school, but much fancier. Large serving bowls of leafy greens, rainbow-coloured vegetables, herby pasta, coleslaw and that grainy stuff that Mum eats – quinoa.

Now, we've been over this before. It's NOT that I'm fussy – I'm just specific. And I don't like things that are too squishy or slimy or wet, but I don't like them dry and hard either. Eating anything my mum hasn't made is a bit hit and miss. I wonder if she'd like to travel the world with me as my personal chef when I finally hit the big time. In the end, I helped myself to some wholemeal pasta and a small dollop of tuna sweetcorn, with garlic bread on the side.

I joined my friends at the table in the corner they'd grabbed. Jaz, as usual, had piled up a tower of food on her plate.

'Food is fuel for football,' she said with a shrug as she bit into a slice of pizza. 'The more

I practise, the more ready I'll be for the Soccer School scouts session. Imagine – I could be invited to trials for a summer academy camp! And then I'll get to meet other girls as footie mad as me.' She chewed on her pizza thoughtfully. 'No offence to you lot,' she added hastily.

'None taken,' said Steph with a smile as she picked at her grapes from a small wooden bowl. Everyone in our team knew that Jaz was the most into football. While we all really liked the beautiful game, Jaz lived and breathed it!

'Is anyone else hoping to get a place in Soccer School?' I asked.

'Not me,' said Naomie. 'My parents have already signed me up for a junior STEM camp at a local university. It's going to be incredible learning more about Pythagoras and the laws of science.'

As boring as that sounded to me, I knew Naomie would love it so I was happy for her.

'I'll be on holiday then. Dad has built up some air miles from his business trips, so we'll be visiting Malaysia, Singapore and Vietnam,' Layla said.

Now *that* sounded fun! Layla explained how her dad got points for travelling for his job. It was a bit like the points on a supermarket card, but instead of free groceries he got money off flights. How cool was that?

'Lucky you,' I said. 'My parents said we can't travel for FOREVER, or at least until the babies stop dribbling and burping everywhere.'

'They're boys, so yeah, that does sound like forever,' said Jaz jokingly. 'So no one else wants to attend Soccer School? There *must* be someone!' she squinted her eyes around at everyone.

'I'm thinking of it,' said Allie.

'That's great, Allie!' said Jaz excitedly. 'Don't forget there's a tournament on the last day here. I wonder if we'll be in the same team. If not, it'll be practice for the future. Imagine if you were the goalie for Chelsea, Allie, and I was a striker for Arsenal!'

'I'd feel really guilty when I saved goals,' Allie said with a cheeky wink.

'In your dreams,' sang Jaz.

'Seriously, though, even if one day we find ourselves in different teams, different jobs, different cities – maybe even different countries – we'll always be the Dream Team, right?' I said.

'Definitely,' said Steph. 'And, for now, let's make the most of the activities and training on offer this week so we can become as good as possible! Then, when we go back to Bramrock, we're bound to top the league because we're the Dream Team!'

'Yay!' said Layla, stretching out her hand across the table.

Everyone put their hands on top, then we lowered them slightly and raised them back up, chanting, '*Dreamers!*'

I couldn't wait to get started!

14

The Blue Oasis

After lunch, there was a short walk from the lodge to the lake where a big white boat, the *Blue Oasis*, was waiting for us.

Mr Roundtree had told us that the students from the other school staying at the lodge, Pennington Academy, would be joining us for the boat ride. I felt a little wobbly getting on, but I got a seat at the front with the Dreamers, then a few minutes later the pupils from Pennington joined us. Most of them filled the seats at the other side of the boat, and some went upstairs to the top deck where most of the Rovers had gone. Then we were off, and the water below us frothed white and blue as the boat sped along.

Our captain, a seafarer called Pascal, who had moved to the New Forest from France, told us all about the marine ecosystem, and how the council had run a major anti-pollution campaign. Their mission? To maintain the pristine lakes and let the fish thrive, he said. Steph was especially enthralled and moved seats nearer to Pascal with Naomie and Talia to ask questions about marine life and environmental issues affecting the oceans.

Seeing that extra spaces had opened up at the front, three girls from Pennington Academy moved over and introduced themselves. Annaliese, Kezia and Tilly were Year 7s, and their team nickname was 'the Pennies'.

'How long have you all played football for? Did you play in primary school?' I asked.

'Three years,' said Kezia.

'Tilly and I didn't have a girls' primary-school team, and the boys would just take over the school pitch, so this is our first year,' explained Annaliese.

'Snap!' said Jaz. 'The Bramrock Rovers didn't want us to join them but we created our own team, which is much better anyway,' she added. 'We haven't played as a team for very long, but we're still the first football team to bring home a trophy for our school in ages!'

'Yeah, we've only just started, so we'll be pros by the time we get to your age,' Allie boasted.

'*Our age?*' gasped Tilly in mock horror. 'You make it sound as if we're really old.'

'Take that as a compliment,' said Layla sweetly. 'We volunteer at our local nursing home, and the old people are so lovely.'

We all laughed, but Layla was right. It isn't a terrible thing to be old. Old people are as interesting and as funny as anyone else. *Maybe even more so*, I thought, remembering all the fascinating stories Betty had told me.

'Do any of you want to play professionally?' asked Kezia.

'I don't,' said Layla.

'Me and Ally might do,' said Jaz. 'We're hoping to get a position in the pre-academy training this summer. A scout is coming to one of our games in April.'

'You don't mess about, do you? Started a team last year and trying to get into an academy this one!' Annaliese said, sounding impressed.

'We just need to impress the scouts. The game they're coming to is one we're playing against our rivals,' Jaz said, looking stressed just thinking about it.

'Jaz is too modest,' I said. 'They'll be lining up to sign her!'

'What about you?' said Annaliese. She looked at me curiously. 'You don't even seem the type to play football.'

Jaz gave her a strange look. 'There isn't just one type of person who can play football, you know. Not in our team anyway. We're all different, and that's why we're the Dream Team!'

I frowned. It was a bit of a weird thing to say, but maybe I wasn't your typical girl footballer, whatever that was. And, considering I was the worst player on the team, perhaps it was a good thing if there weren't many other footballers like me.

'I like football,' I said. 'It's a lot of fun, but I'm not nearly good enough to try out for Soccer School. Plus, I have no intention of becoming a professional footballer – although I wouldn't mind being something like a sports broadcaster one day.'

'I couldn't think of anything worse than talking in front of millions of people,' said Tilly, shuddering.

'That's where you're different from our Charligh,' said Allie with a grin. 'She loves being in the spotlight. That's why she's the lead in the Year Six musical-theatre production this year.'

'That's so cool,' exclaimed Kezia. 'I love singing, but I just stick to doing it in the bath.'

'Give us a song then,' said Annaliese, who I was discovering was the bossy one of the trio.

I wasn't going to be ordered about by anyone, but I would also never miss out on an opportunity to show off my voice. So, as the *Blue Oasis* sailed round the lake, Layla got 'Let it Go' from *Frozen* up on her tablet, since I thought that suited the icy-cold afternoon. I hadn't realized I was singing so loudly until the end when everyone on deck clapped – so I sang it one more time!

*

That evening, after dinner, everyone gathered in the lounge to play board games. But I went up to the dormitory early and got ready for bed. I needed my beauty sleep! Then I called home to say goodnight. Mum answered on the first ring.

'Hi, Charligh! Are you OK?'

'Of course she is, Viv,' I heard Dad say in the background. She'd put me on speakerphone.

'What Dad said,' I said, smiling. 'This place is beautiful. It looks even grander and more –' I searched for the word – '*picturesque* than on the website. You'd both love it – it's full of history and art and books. It was built hundreds of years ago and it's a Grade One listed building,' I said.

'That *is* right up my street, Charligh. I'll go and fetch the twins.' Dad's voice sounded a bit more distant, like he was walking away from the phone, then a few seconds later I heard the familiar sound of Rory and Reuben chatting and babbling away. 'They're rubbish on the phone. Shall we do video?'

I turned on my video and saw the smiling faces of Rory and Reuben, who are always thrilled by the sight of people they know on a screen. Rory was chatting away as usual, but Reuben reached over and touched the screen, then looked surprised and a bit hurt that it was just hard plastic. He burst out into a long, wailing cry that I usually find annoying, but tonight made me feel a bit rotten.

Dad hugged him tight. 'Don't worry, your favourite person will be back soon, just five more sleeps.' Dad tickled his feet, which made him laugh again.

I showed my family the room I was in, turning the camera away and describing everything, including the view from the window, as if I was doing a documentary. I eventually panned back to me and said, 'And this is where I sleep,' gesturing over my shoulder.

'Great tour,' said Mum. 'Where's Jaz? Where are all your team-mates?'

'Don't worry, I haven't scared them off yet,' I said, laughing. 'They'll be coming up in a bit. They're downstairs playing games, but I was feeling a bit tired. Plus, I want to learn my lines,' I added.

'I'm very proud of you, Charligh,' Dad said. 'You're showing such commitment to memorizing your part. Now you just need to apply that dedication to doing your homework on time – even your maths!'

I rolled my eyes. 'I should have known you'd find a way to bring homework into it.'

Mum lowered her voice. 'The twins are falling asleep . . . I think it's the excitement of seeing their big sister. So we'll say goodbye and get them to bed. All the best with learning your lines. Can I say break a leg, or is it too early?'

'Thanks, Mum,' I said, smiling. I blew kisses at the twins, even though by this point their eyes had shut completely.

'Love you, Charligh.'

'Love you too,' I said as I ended the call, and their picture left my screen.

The next morning I was the first one to wake up. I got out of bed and looked at my phone: it was 7 a.m., and the sun was just rising. Very quietly, I slid my script off the bedside table and put on my Crocs and dressing gown, stuffing the script into one of the pockets. But as I moved towards the door . . . I tripped over Jaz's football studs. *Ouch!*

For some reason, she had tipped the contents of her sports bag on to the floor, probably making sure she had everything ready for the training session that began after breakfast at 9:30 sharp. It was a bit like the carpet of clothes in my room, but at least there I knew where everything was, not like here where it was all strange and unfamiliar and likely to trip me up.

'*Shh!*' hissed Talia from her bunk.

And thanks for the heart-warming sympathy, I thought as I rubbed my toes gingerly.

'I thought I was the only one awake,' I said in my most discreet whisper. 'Since you're up, how about we go down and explore Meaden Lodge?'

'Explore where?' said Talia, looking suspicious. I could just visualize it – a list of rules scrolling up and down in her mind.

'I'm not going to leave the building, if that's what you think. I just meant let's have a look downstairs,' I said.

'No, I'm going back to sleep,' came the muffled reply as Talia turned her back to me.

Fine – suit yourself, I thought, relieved to escape her grumbling and eagle eyes.

15

An Uphill Journey

The canteen area was locked up with the silver shutters down. I sat at a table near the floor-to-ceiling windows, watching the sunrise dance on the lake. I'd have thought anything so quiet and still would be dull, but sitting there, watching the sun make its grand arrival, was anything but.

I started going through my script, and – to my relief – the words were slowly becoming more familiar. I know Allie had scoffed, but this lake was wonderful, and I really could imagine I was Anne with an 'e' now.

I clasped my hands together and went through the scene where Anne begs the Cuthberts not to send her away.

It'd be so much easier and more fun if I could have my script with me when we put on the play, I thought. But that was for amateurs, and I was DEFINITELY not one of those.

I put the script down on a side table and tried to recite my lines from memory ... but immediately forgot them again. I slumped down on a nearby seat.

'Do I get front-row tickets?' Jaz said, startling me.

I jumped up. 'Don't scare me like that! I didn't hear you come in. Were you tiptoeing or something?'

'Nope,' she said, sitting down next to me. 'I guess you were just lost in the world of Anne Shirley. This must be really bugging you for you to get up so early to learn your lines. How long is it until the play again now?'

'Forty-two days. That's, like, six weeks away.' I sighed.

Jaz picked up the script from the side table where I'd put it. 'I'll be your line prompter.

Repeat as much as you can, and, when you get stuck, I'll help you out. Where are we starting?'

'From the beginning,' I said grimly.

'Lights, camera, action!' said Jaz.

This time, something started to click into place, and I found myself remembering most of the lines. We managed to get through all the scenes in Act 1 before one of the housekeeping staff rolled in with their cleaning equipment and gave us a stern look.

'I think that's our cue to go,' said Jaz.

I smiled. 'Thanks for helping me. I know you'd rather be out there practising football.'

'That's what besties are for, and I love reading anyway. Although, I'll leave the acting to you,' Jaz said with a grin.

Rhiannon had made it down from Bramrock and joined us at our table for breakfast, showing us all the different looks she'd presented at the Make-Up and Fashion Showcase at Bramrock College the day before. She'd had a busy week, but was pleased at how it had gone and was now looking forward to the football training and activities.

We had our first football session after breakfast. They put all of us together, the Rovers, the Dreamers and both the Pennies teams. Anders, Elsa and Taheer led the warm-up – stretches and a short jog. Rhiannon and Mr Roundtree gave out yellow bibs that had plastic slots for us to insert our name labels. I very nearly wrote Tallulah because today I felt it would be MAGNIFICENT to be called that, but Steph told me it might get confusing since it wasn't my name. She did have a point, so I settled for my usual Charligh with a 'gh'.

Anders, who was tall with a low, stern voice, said today's session would be concentrating on dribbling. Let's just say that is not my favourite activity, mainly because it often ends with me tripping over my own feet, and the ball doesn't always stick as close to me as I'd like.

'Come on! You can do it, Charligh!' shouted Taheer encouragingly as I dribbled the ball through a line of cones. He was my favourite. He had a broad smile and a multicoloured stripy hat that made me like him immediately.

We then moved on to one-touch passes and relay drills, and then finally they split us into teams, and we each played an eleven vs eleven game just before lunch. It was fun, even though I ended up stuck on a team with Zach and Sebastian. Yuck!

After training, it was time for the nature walk and orienteering. We would begin with a ramble through the countryside followed by a much longer walk after lunch. This sounded straightforward enough, but then Miss Williams dropped a bombshell: we were going to split up, and each group would go to a different starting point from which they would have to find their way back to the lodge using maps and compasses.

'How does getting lost and going round in circles help us with football?' said Sebastian grumpily. For once, I think I agreed with him.

'Can anyone answer that?' said Dodson.

'You can't think of anything else for us to do?' said Zach.

The boys sniggered, falling silent as Rhiannon gave them a cold look.

'Any sensible answers?' Dodson said dryly.

Steph raised her hand. 'So we can trust each other more.'

Rhys, who was a striker for the Pennington Academy boys' team, raised his hand. 'Team building.'

'Both great answers,' Miss Williams said. 'OK, you can go back to your rooms and get ready. Make sure you're wearing your sturdiest and strongest shoes, a waterproof jacket if you have one, and then pick up your packed lunch from the canteen. When we reach the picnic area, we'll stop and have a break. She looked at her watch. 'Let's meet back at reception in forty-five minutes!'

Jaz and Allie were powering ahead with Zach and Sebastian, and I could tell even from the back of their heads that the four of them were making faces behind Mr Roundtree's back. It wasn't a bad idea, and I'd have joined them if it wasn't for the fact I'd have had to speed up.

Steph was in the middle of the group with Naomie, Talia, Theo and Olly. They were pointing out birds and plants and flowers that they'd never seen before so they could learn what they were called. Since we weren't allowed to take our phones, Steph was one of the students given a class camera to take pictures of our ramble through the countryside.

I walked at the back with Layla and two of the three Pennies we'd made friends with on yesterday's boat trip – Annaliese and Kezia.

'Wow, guys! This is some hike,' I said, puffed. I drew in a long, loud and extremely ragged breath for effect, then adjusted the straps on my backpack.

'We've actually not even left Meaden Lodge's grounds,' said Kezia with a giggle.

'You're joking! We'll never survive this!'

'We will too, and it's going to be so much fun,' said Layla. 'An hour is a bit of a long walk, but look how beautiful the journey will be.'

Finally, we reached the gates of Meaden Lodge. Before us stretched a wide road with large open fields and rolling hills on each side.

This is not *my idea of fun at all*, I thought.

16

Finding New Paths

To my astonishment, it appeared Layla was right. Traipsing through the countryside *was* fun after all. After marching down the road from Meaden Lodge, we reached a winding path that ran through some fields and then over a bridge. Before long, we had come to the picnic area, a pretty clearing that had weeping willows all around and tall, twisty trees that leaned over and touched each other, forming a natural canopy above.

The best and most magnificent thing was the melodic, tuneful tinkling from the stream that ran through it. If you looked down into the water like I was doing now, you could see heaps of pebbles in different sizes, shapes and colours – earthy brown, translucent white, dandelion yellow and cranberry red – twinkling and dancing under the sun's bright rays.

'I can't believe how many different flowers and birds I've spotted on this walk. Biodiversity is so beautiful and important,' Steph said as she flicked through the images on her camera, and we settled down to eat our packed lunches.

'Bio what?' said Allie, frowning.

'Biodiversity is basically all the different plants, animals and every form of life you find in an area, including the tiny things that we can't even see without a microscope.'

'Can we just stay here forever?' said Layla with a sigh, flicking sandwich crumbs on to the blankets that covered the wild grass we were sitting on.

As if answering her question, Mr Roundtree blew his whistle, which he insisted on using even off the pitch.

'I hope you have all enjoyed lunch and the scenic views,' he said pleasantly. It was probably the most cheerful thing he'd ever said to us. The countryside air was clearly doing him good too. 'Now we're splitting into teams of four again – to make it easier, form the same ones you were in for this morning's games.'

Now the FANTABULOUS thing about this was that I had Jaz, Naomie and Steph in my team as well as Kezia and Annaliese. The Not So Fantabulous thing is that Dodson was supervising us. I did quietly suggest to Rhiannon that she swap with him, but she gave me a rather hard look.

Dodson explained the task to us after we'd assembled our team. The adult supervisor (him) would lead us to a spot twenty minutes away, and then we'd pick a leader from our team who'd use the map and compass to find our way back to Meaden Lodge. On the route, we'd pass three checkpoints and collect a flag from each one.

When we got to our starting point, I rather bravely volunteered to be the team leader. I wasn't the most experienced at this kind of thing, but as Daphne Dabello said, 'Fake it till you make it.' No one could tell that you didn't have a clue what you were doing as long as you made them believe that you could do it. This was a perfect time to put my acting skills into action.

Where we stood now was much higher than the stream of coloured pebbles, and below us was a green patchwork of fields. All we had to do was find the path that continued into Meaden Woods.

'Are you sure you want to lead us back?' Dodson said.

'Yes, I'm sure,' I said rather forcefully. Well, he had asked me the same question twice in the space of one minute.

He rubbed his forehead and scrunched up his nose in that rabbit-like way of his. 'This is a group effort. Is there anyone else who wants to co-lead with Charligh?'

Steph put her hand up. 'I will,' she said cheerfully. 'Why don't you give me the map since you have the compass?'

Not so fast!

I loved Steph, of course, but being the big sister of three brothers, and also school captain last term, had made her a LITTLE bossy, and I wanted this win for myself.

'*You* can take the compass,' I said, firmly grasping the map.

But, well ... after an hour of aimless wandering, it became clear that I'd maybe exaggerated the usefulness of faking it while overlooking the importance of actually having a sense of direction.

'I'm sure we've been by that same willow tree twice,' said Olly with a sigh.

'We've actually passed it *three* times. Sorry, but we're definitely going round in circles,' said Naomie.

'We're going to get caught in the rain, and we've only picked up one flag,' said Zach crossly. 'You're rotten at this. Trust you *Dreamers* to get us lost.'

Jaz and I stuck our tongues out at him in perfect sync.

I stared hard at the map until I felt Steph tapping me on the shoulder. 'Charligh, the map's the wrong way round.' She looked at her compass. 'East is DEFINITELY that way.' She pointed in the opposite direction to where I was facing.

I quickly turned the map round, hoping no one else would notice, but it was too late.

'If this is a map-reading exercise, we probably need someone who can actually read a map?' Kezia said politely.

'I *was* reading it! I was just looking at it from a different perspective. It's something I've been learning to do as a young thespian,' I said rather loudly, hoping to impress Dodson.

'A what?' asked Kezia.

'It's a fancy name for actor,' said Jaz.

'It IS going to rain, Charligh,' Dodson said. 'But the choice belongs to you and your team.'

I was beginning to feel that I couldn't even convince even myself that this was part of my orienteering strategy when we heard the rumble of far-off thunder. So, to avoid an unseemly takeover, I reluctantly admitted defeat and handed the map over to Steph for her to lead us back. It turned out to be the right decision since she very quickly got us on the right path, and we managed to collect the remaining two flags.

We spent the last five minutes rushing through Meaden Woods before the heavens opened, and we managed to get back just in the nick of time.

However, we weren't too surprised to find out we were the fourth and last team to return to Meaden Lodge, but still . . . At least we'd completed the orienteering course.

After dinner we played board games, and then we got ready for bed. Miss Williams was on bedtime duty and, about half an hour after she'd made sure we were safely tucked up, we all snuck out of bed, except for Allie, who was sleeping like a log. We'd decided to have a midnight feast. I wished I could say it was my brainchild, but Jaz was actually the genius behind this idea. I think she was inspired by all those boarding-school stories she reads about girls sneaking off to share snacks after lights-out.

To avoid getting caught by any adults patrolling the corridor, we kept the main light off, but opened the curtains a little so the moon shone in and we used the lights on our phones to illuminate the room as we gathered round a pile of half-eaten coach snacks.

'It's not exactly a midnight feast,' said Talia, tutting. She pointed at the time on Jaz's phone. 'It's ten fifty-three.'

'Well, it's an almost-midnight feast then, Talia,' I said enthusiastically, sticking my hand into a huge bag of cheesy Wotsits. Unlike Talia, I wasn't one to split hairs, and whatever you called this I was enjoying it!

'Isn't the storm loud and a bit spooky?' said Layla, her quiet voice almost overpowered by the rising grumble of thunder and the wailing of the wind.

I stood up and pressed my nose against the window. It was damp with condensation. I gazed out over the lake just as a flash of lightning streaked through the sky, which did look eerie. Layla was right: it was like something out of a horror movie, and I loved it.

I spun round. 'Why don't we tell ghost stories?' I suggested.

'I don't think that's a good idea. What if it scares Layla?' Jaz said.

'I'm not scared,' said Layla indignantly.

'Who wants to start?' asked Naomie.

'I will,' said Steph. She told us a not-very-frightening story about a girl who hears voices in her attic and then finds out it's a bird's nest.

'There is literally nothing scary about that story,' I said.

Layla shrugged. 'Well, it has a happy ending and that's the main thing,' she said, looking relieved that she hadn't been terrified.

I tried not to roll my eyes at my friends and instead offered to go next. I'd show them what a real ghost story was all about. So I began to spin a tale that was a mix of stories I'd heard before and new ones that were forming in my head the more I looked out at the lake. It was a very long and complicated story involving a headless alien, a fire-breathing seahorse and the jealous younger sibling of a kind and talented countess.

It got so spooky and unpredictable with all the unhappy accidents I kept filling the story with that, in the end, it wasn't Layla shivering under her blankets, it was me. My story had been so long that we managed to finish all the snacks, but were now either exhausted, or completely terrified, or in my case BOTH! So our almost-midnight feast didn't quite make it to twelve, but I now knew that late-night storytelling in a medieval castle in the middle of a storm is scarier than the scariest of movies.

The next day the weather was still miserable so we all trooped across to the lodge's fancy all-purpose modern building that had an indoor sports hall, a swimming pool and a fitness gym. Training was even harder than yesterday, and Anders was particularly intense, but somehow we got through it in one piece. I was feeling especially exhilarated, though, because that morning I'd managed to get up early again for the second time in a row.

This time there was no Jaz to help me learn my lines – I think she was still exhausted from our almost-midnight feast – but I found a spot in the lounge and practised my lines for a whole hour. Finally, they seemed to be sinking in, although I didn't actually get past the first act again, but I was fully confident I'd be able to move on to Act 2 tomorrow.

For our afternoon activity, I had chosen the poetry workshop instead of swimming. Truth be told, I didn't want to embarrass myself with yellow armbands. Nearly everyone had opted for swimming, so the class consisted of me, Talia, Layla, Olly and two Pennies called Marcus and Seren.

'Does anyone know what haikus are?' Dodson said as he perched on the edge of a large, grand-looking table in the conference lounge.

Layla's hand shot up. 'It's a type of poetry that originated in Japan, made up of three short sentences that don't rhyme.'

Dodson scribbled Layla's haiku explanation on a flipchart. 'Correct, Layla – and also very important, the first line has five syllables, the second has seven and the third has five. Have you or anyone here ever written a haiku?'

I wanted to say yes to impress Dodson, but I knew, with his forensic attention to detail, he'd ask me to recite one so I was smart enough to say nothing.

Layla flipped through her fluffy pink journal. 'I have, but I'd rather not share,' she said, her voice dropping to barely a whisper.

'I can read it out for you,' I offered valiantly.

Layla clutched her journal to her chest protectively.

'Poetry is very personal. She might not want to share what she's written with the whole class,' Olly said.

'Um, OK,' I said. *Sheesh*. It was only three little lines!

Dodson set us the task of writing our first haiku after he'd read out some more examples. My first one wasn't very good. It was about a man travelling to work and forgetting his cheese sandwiches. I stared at the page blankly.

'Goodness me, are you lost for words, Charligh?' Dodson said with a smile as he came over and pulled up a stool next to my desk. 'Why don't you write about something you're really interested in? I find art that comes from the heart is the easiest to write, and it's the most impactful.'

I thought about all the things I could write about – movies, plays, cats – and finally decided on something I missed – Sandy's ring doughnuts.

Dodson let us read ours out if we wanted, and everyone did, even Layla. When it came to my turn, I felt a bit silly because everyone had written beautiful ones about winter days or summer sunrises or wild animals, and mine was about a doughnut.

> '*Yum! Berry doughnuts*
> *From our Saturday market*
> *Are sweet and magic.*'

But Dodson said it was great, and you could see the love I had for doughnuts shining through. Olly sniggered at this, but I think it was a really nice thing for Dodson to say.

'This is just one form of poetry,' Dodson said at the end of the class. 'Poetry can come in many forms – rhyming, free verse, narrative, spoken word and much more – but the most important thing is that it comes from your heart – because what is your art if it doesn't come from the heart?' he said with a chuckle.

'You're a poet and you don't even know it!' called out Seren.

'We're all poets,' said Layla firmly.

I wasn't so sure, but I did like the idea of adding 'poet' to my list of creative talents. 'Charligh Green, poet and actor' did have a nice ring to it!

17

Goodbyes

The next morning we were back on the outdoor pitch for more training. It seemed they were giving us an easier day in the lead-up to the final tournament tomorrow. There were no more dribbling drills. Hurrah! Honestly, what a tongue-twister: hard to say and even harder to do. We played a lot of new football games. My two favourites were Steal the Tail, which helped improve our ability to twist, turn and shake off the people marking us, and Baller in the Middle, which was good practice for our passing and interception skills.

'Great session. I hope you're all ready for the tournament tomorrow,' Elsa said.

'We have been practising all week!' said Kezia.

'I mean mentally prepared.' Elsa tapped the side of her head. 'So many players don't attain their full potential because they're distracted, or their head just isn't in the game. Anyway, I'll pass you over to Rhiannon now. She's going to explain this afternoon's activity choices.'

I knew exactly what they were. I'd been looking forward to the paddleboarding!

Rhiannon came over to the middle of our group. 'Thanks, Elsa. Well, it's a choice between paddleboarding or arts and crafts. We'll be using life jackets, of course, and staying in the shallow end of the water, but if you're not able to swim please let us know, and a specialist instructor can go on the paddleboard with you.'

Needless to say, I chose arts and crafts, despite being pretty rubbish at both of those things. Me and Allie were the only Dreamers who'd chosen that option, so it was us two, as well as Olly,

Ricardo and about five Pennies from both the boys' and girls' teams.

Allie got straight to work, making rows of origami paper cranes on which she sketched the prettiest and most intricate designs. I'd always known she had a thing for art, but I hadn't realized how brilliant she was at it.

From the craft activities on offer, I'd chosen to make a masquerade-style mask. Elsa said that many years ago, in a big house like this, the lord and lady of the manor would have had all their fancy friends round for masquerade balls – which she explained was a fancy word for costume parties – where they wore beautiful eye masks to disguise themselves.

I made a white-and-silver glittery one with a wooden stick so I could hold it up and look through it. I absolutely loved it and knew it would come in handy during the shows that I put on for the Tinies.

'I'm glad to see the artist inside being unlocked,' said Miss Williams, smiling.

A poet and an artist and *an actor*, I thought as we packed up and went to join the others, who were coming back in from the paddleboarding activity. I definitely liked the sound of that.

The next day – our last full day! – we rounded up a week of football training with a seven-a-side tournament. We'd been divided into teams. I was terribly excited, not only because I was convinced that my team were destined to win the trophy, but also because our name – the Incredibles – was one I'd come up with, and everyone loved it. As if that wasn't enough, we had rainbow-coloured bibs. Our team, our name, our strip – it was all truly incredible.

Anders blew the whistle at the end of our first game, and the Incredibles all high-fived each other after an effortless 4–0 win against the badly named Champions team, whose second defeat in a row meant they were out of the tournament.

Twenty minutes later, it was time for our second match against the Smarties. 'Is everyone clear on what we need to do?'

Naomie nodded. 'We're switching sides.'

'To confuse their markers,' added Kezia.

It sounded like a perfect idea, and I'd chimed in with my approval when Olly had run it by us the first time, but now I was worried that I'd be the one getting confused. Let's face it, it didn't take much to trip me up on the pitch. I could just see it now: my legs getting all tangled and clumped together like wet spaghetti.

We had everything to play for – if we won this game, our place in the final would be secured. As Zach, who was the striker for the Smarties, ran down the wing, Skye, who was super fast, got in his path and took possession of the ball, then started kicking it ahead of her towards me. I ran over to the right side and saw Zach's look of frustration. I could tell that he was torn between playing on the left side and chasing the ball, or relying on Talia, which I knew he wouldn't like since she plays football differently to him.

While Zach was figuring it out, Skye pushed the ball up to Rhys, who kicked it on to Steph in the middle of the pitch. All the Smarties moved towards her. She ran to the opposite side, then back-heeled it suddenly to Olly, who'd switched to her side, causing confusion at the front. Then Olly snuck a goal in while everyone was figuring out who they were marking now, and what side they wanted to be on . . . and we scored the first and last goal of the match. 1–0 to the Incredibles! We were through to the final!

So . . . we played the Goldies in the final. I won't give you all the details, mainly because they involve the Goldies running circles around us, but let's just say the final outcome was that we lost, so it didn't go quite as planned. I also didn't get near the ball all match, so I felt a bit like an actor waiting in the wings or someone backstage watching the real drama unfold. It wasn't my favourite type of game, and, oh yeah, we didn't even score a goal – we lost 2–0. On the bright side, it was Jaz who scored both of them. Out of all the boys and girls, my BBF was still the top goal scorer – now that was something to cheer about! And second place wasn't bad. At least we still got special medals along with the certificates every player was awarded for participating.

'Congratulations to you all,' Miss Williams said after she presented the Goldies with their first-place medals. 'Whether you came first, second or third, or didn't get a place, be proud of your participation certificates. You came here to bond with your team, acquire new skills and learn discipline, and for that you should be proud. It's all about the journey, not the destination, and, if we all remember that, we'll really improve not just in football but in anything we do.'

The only sad part was saying goodbye to the Pennies. They had arrived the night before us and were leaving a night earlier too, since their town, Pennington, near Bournemouth, was only an hour away. We exchanged phone numbers and email addresses with our three favourite Pennies – Kezia, Annaliese and Tilly – and promised to keep in touch. They even said they'd subscribe to the *Charligh Green Show* so, as sad as it was, OF COURSE, to say bye to our new friends, at least I'd gained three new fans for my channel!

18

Fireside Tales

To celebrate our last night, the Meaden Lodge staff and our teachers had set up the outdoor table section with heaters that glowed warm yellow in the gentle evening darkness. I wore a long, white, bohemian lace-trimmed dress with my black-and-red Converse trainers, and sat at a table with Jaz, Steph and Naomie. Layla, Allie and Talia were on the next one along. In the centre of all the tables was an electric barbecue.

'I think we should play a get-to-know-you game,' said Mr Roundtree.

Huh? We'd spent all week getting to know each other. But Miss Williams nodded. 'The Rovers know each other as a team very well, and the Dreamers do too, but I'm not sure how well you know each other!' she said with a smile.

The Rovers were crowded round the two tables opposite us, and we all looked suspiciously at one another.

'I have an idea,' said Dodson. 'I often play this with drama groups. Two truths and a lie. You tell two truths and one lie, and we have to guess which one is a lie. Ladies first, so I'll let Miss Williams begin, and then Rhiannon and the Dreamers can go next.'

'OK, two truths and one lie,' Miss Williams began. 'I've been growing my locs for seven years, I used to live in Spain and I'm scared of flying.'

'I think you're lying about being scared of flying, miss!' said Zach straight away. 'You told us you used to live in Spain in the first week of term, and your dreadlocks are SUPER long, so I can believe you've been growing them for seven years.'

'Correct,' said Miss Williams, smiling.

'I can't believe how long Miss Williams has been growing her hair,' said Jaz.

'I can't believe Zach actually said something intelligent,' I whispered back.

As we each took a turn, I found out so much about the Rovers. Ricardo has a brother who's twenty and in the army who he misses a lot. Olly learned to code over the holidays and is in the process of building a website, and Sebastian has broken his left leg three times in three different places. He must be even clumsier than I am!

For my two truths and a lie, I said I wanted to be a famous actor, I'd met the Queen and I had my own YouTube channel. Everyone knew the second one was the lie!

I even learned new things about some of the Dreamers. I found out Allie's uncle was teaching her to play Djembe drums. It did make sense – Allie was so quick and clever with her hands, and she was always drumming out a beat on a chair or table.

That night, our last, was the best one. Warming our hands over the heater, drinking creamy hot chocolate dotted with sweet, soft marshmallows, singing songs, clapping our hands to keep time and keep warm, learning new football chants that rang into the night air . . .

And, just like that, our adventure in the New Forest was over, and we were waving goodbye frantically to Anders, Taheer, Elsa, Mr Kerrigan and all the other Meaden Lodge staff as we buckled up in the coach. The Rovers had beaten us to the back seats this time, but I was quite happy to be at the front anyway, and I suppose it was only fair not to hog the same seats on both journeys. I had more important things to do – like writing to my pen pal Betty! I had so much to tell her.

Dear Betty,

I hope you are well. Meaden Lodge castle was the absolute best! I had a few minor upsets, though: getting everyone lost, not quite getting the hang of haiku poetry, plus mistakenly waking people up before dawn just because the excitement got me up early every day.

I was utterly determined to learn my lines, and I did memorize an awful lot of them, even though

Dodson didn't ask me about it once. Yes, would you believe it – he actually came along on our football trip, which was a bit of a not-so-nice surprise, but he ended up being actually kind of nice.

Anyway, back to the lines thing. While I wouldn't say they've started to flow, a little trickle has begun, and it does feel like a weight's been lifted. I may have started out a caterpillar, but I'm well on my way to getting my butterfly wings.

Sorry if my words are ~~indeciphr~~ indecipherable. The road is getting bumpier, and it's making my ~~handwritting~~ handwriting even messier, so I think now would be a good time to end this letter.

Love and drama,

Charligh Green

*

'How are you finding everything, Charligh? Are you coping OK with rehearsals and learning your lines?' Miss Williams had asked me to stay behind for a few minutes when everyone rolled out for morning break on Wednesday.

'Of course!' I exclaimed.

She didn't look convinced. Perhaps I'd been a tad overenthusiastic. I decided to take it down a notch.

'Well, OK, it's not been super easy, but I'm definitely the right person to play Anne.'

I KNEW Summer had slithered all snake-like up to Miss Williams and dropped me right in it. She probably dressed it up as concern and said something about taking the main part off my hands. Of course, I hadn't heard any of this, but I knew Summer was sly, and the timing was too convenient.

Just last night after school, the rehearsal had gone pretty badly. Despite the play being exactly five weeks, seven hours and forty-two minutes away now, ALL the lines I'd learned when I was away seemed to have disappeared from my memory, almost as if I'd dropped them at the bottom of the Meaden Lodge lake.

Miss Williams smiled. 'I'm sure you are. Anything worth doing is never easy, but if you need any help, please let me know. I realize that, on top of the performance, you and the Dreamers have been dropping into Flora House most weeks, not to mention the big game against the Shiners, which is important for more reasons than one.'

'No biggie,' I said breezily, even though, when she listed everything like that, it did sound RATHER A LOT.

'I've mentioned this to your parents already, but we have an educational psychologist visiting the school this month, and I've put you forward to be assessed because I think you'd benefit from it. If nothing else, they can help you examine the best ways for you to learn and how we can all support you better.'

I frowned inside, quietly resolving to make sure I'd learned my lines before the appointment so I could (very politely, of course) tell this educational psychologist person I didn't need any 'support'. But I knew that, when adults offered help, if you shot it down too quickly, it kind of became a THING that they pushed for even harder. So I just smiled and nodded before heading out of the classroom. But, deep inside, I knew I couldn't mess up my first real shot on the stage, or I'd become the class clown, the joke of the town and a complete pariah. (OK, maybe I'm exaggerating with that last one, but I heard it said in a film, and it sounded dramatically horrific.) OR ... even worse, everyone would just feel sorry for me, and I HATED that. I needed to take DRASTIC action before everything toppled over with a CRASH.

Naomie's dad was like the grown-up boy version of Naomie, tall with serious dark eyes and the same perfect Colgate smile, which he was wearing now as he opened the door to me.

So, when I had told the Dreamers I needed a tiny sprinkle of help, Naomie and Steph said they were they free that evening, and I decided to take them up on it. Now, here I was at Naomie's house after school on Wednesday.

'Come in!' said Mr Osei as he stepped back from the door. He was holding a large bucket in one hand. Effie was peeking round her dad's legs and pretending to be shy when really she was anything but. Today she was wearing a sparkling tiara, a pink-and-white T-shirt and a shimmery pink tutu. She couldn't have been more glitzy if she tried. Her hair was twisted into six braids with brightly coloured jumbo beads at the end of each one.

Effie and I are Birthday Twins, though she was born four years after me, on 14 May. Last year, Naomie had invited me, Steph and Jaz to Effie's Disney-themed fancy-dress birthday party. Effie loves dressing up. She has a bunch of different styles and is always coming up with ideas for new looks. Effie sort of reminds me of me when I was her age. OK, she reminds me of me now as well.

'I'm a *meevil* princess, Charligh,' she said with a grin, showing two missing front teeth as she ran and hugged me round the waist.

Her full name is Efua, and she insists on being known as that in school, but everyone in her family calls her Effie, and she said I could call her that too since I'm her Birthday Twin.

'*Me-di-eval*,' Naomie corrected her from the top of the stairs. 'And that is not how they used to dress, Effie.'

'You're the best-dressed meevil princess ever,' I told her. Seriously, I LOVED her style. Who wants to wear the same as everyone else when you can stand out?

Naomie's dad smiled. 'Effie loved hearing about and seeing pictures of Meaden Lodge, so she's decided to learn more about the medieval period,' he said as he disentangled his youngest daughter from my waist in one swift move, hoisting her up for a piggyback. 'Now this royal person is going to help her lowly father wash the car,' he said as he stepped out of the front door.

'Bye, Effie,' I said.

Effie fluttered one of her chubby hands in a queenly wave as her dad ambled off with her on his back and the bucket in his hand.

Naomie closed the door behind them. 'Good, now the noise is out of the house we can get on with learning those lines!'

The theme of Naomie's room decoration represents one of her biggest passions. She wants to be an astronaut, or an astronomer . . . I think, or maybe it's an astrophysicist? It's an astro-something anyway, that much I'm sure of, and astro means it's related to outer space, which she knows a zillion-trillion facts about. The walls are an earthy blue-grey, with planets made of soft wood hanging from the ceiling, and the light bulb in the centre of her room is covered with a huge sun-like shade. She also has this special light in the corner that throws up tiny starlike dots on the ceiling when the room is dark, and next to her window is a grey telescope on a stand.

If you don't think those things exist outside of schools, museums and movies, Naomie is there to prove you wrong. I'd taken a peek through it once, hoping I'd see aliens or something exciting, but all I spotted was a close-up of a neighbour's roof. She said her telescope was for looking at nebulae and galaxies and comets on clear dark nights. I don't really know what any of those words mean, but the only stars I'm interested in are the ones on the West End stage or on the sets of Hollywood movies.

Steph was already there, sitting on the bed. Naomie sat on the other side, her long legs crossed under her.

'We can't wait to get started, Charligh,' Steph said, taking her script out of a plastic folder and smoothing it down. 'Jaz is coming later. She'll be here in about an hour. I think she's off doing research on women's football clubs for the presentation next term. I'm doing mine on climate change and what the world needs to do to save the planet – I've found loads online already. When are you starting yours?'

I sat down between them, feeling slightly apprehensive – they were both so serious when it came to learning.

'Probably the night before, knowing me,' I said honestly.

I've never been much good at starting things on time. I always have the best of intentions, but I usually do my homework at the last minute, no matter how many reminders everyone gives me.

Unlike her best friend, Steph doesn't have dreams of going into space – sensible Steph has her feet firmly on the ground and wants to be a teacher. It sounds like the worst thing in the world to me, and because she's one of my closest friends I even sent her a picture of the piles of marking my mum had to do over the 'holidays' in an effort to warn her, but she actually looked EXCITED about it.

'So?' said Naomie.

Oops. Naomie must have been talking to me, but how was I supposed to know precisely what she'd said when I hadn't actually been listening?

Ugh. Some days it feels like people expected the impossible of me.

'We were asking exactly how much of this you've learned. The first two acts?' Steph said.

I hesitated.

Steph narrowed her eyes. 'The first act?' she said slowly.

'Well . . . to be honest, I haven't really learned much beyond, "I can't tell you how excited I am. I'm the luckiest, most grateful and happiest girl on this entire island, I promise you, Mr Cuthbert."'

They looked at me as if waiting for me to go on. I shrugged guiltily as Naomie's rocket-shaped clock ticked loudly in the background.

'Is that all you've learned, Charligh?' Naomie gasped. 'That's like the opening scene of the first act after your song. We've been practising for almost a month, and the final is on –' she flipped a page on her desk calendar so it displayed the month of March – 'March the twenty-eighth, which is twenty-eight days away – just five weeks.'

Wow! And people said I was the drama queen. Some of us just take our time to learn this stuff. Let the lines marinate, right?

'I know what twenty-eight days is in weeks, Naomie. And I do know a bit more than that – it's just hard to keep it all in my head. And, anyway, I've been busy,' I said evasively.

'Busy doing what?' asked Steph.

'You know, just busy things,' I said vaguely, thinking of the hours spent watching Daphne Dabello reruns, trying out different vintage looks, recording videos for the *Charligh Green Show* and putting on impromptu shows for the Tinies.

'Plus, not everyone is a superbrain like you, Naomie,' I added defensively.

'I'm not a superbrain. I just make sure I learn whatever I need to, and *you* need to learn your lines, Charligh,' Naomie said, frowning.

'You'll get frown lines,' I said helpfully.

'*What?*'

'Frown lines. They'll stick if you keep doing that.'

'Not everyone is concerned about wrinkles, Charligh, and we're only ten years old,' she said earnestly. 'And honestly the skin's capacity for regeneration and renewal is incredible, especially at our young age.'

Ugh. I should have known Naomie would ram in some boring science fact. Despite not seeming to care much about beauty, she has long thick eyelashes framing big dark eyes, a button nose, and she's pretty, like ... stop-and-stare movie-star beautiful. Everyone thinks she'll win the Year 6 STEM prize – her nickname is MENSA because she's a total whizz at maths in addition to being a science geek.

'Fine, frown away, Naomie – just don't say I didn't warn you,' I said, throwing my hands up.

Steph sighed. 'OK, let's start from the beginning, Charligh. I'll be Matthew Cuthbert and Diana, and Naomie can do the lines for Marilla Cuthbert and Gilbert.'

We read through the first act twice, then it was time to do it without my script.

'So this is the Lake of Shining Waters,' I said after Naomie had finished Matthew Cuthbert's speech. And then ... nothing.

I knew there was more – I had literally just been reading the lines – but somehow the words had slipped out of my head as if they had dropped into the Lake of Shining Waters.

I chewed the inside of my lip. 'You know, I could do with some water,' I said, trying to delay the inevitable by making Naomie pop downstairs.

I was sure Naomie was trying hard not to roll her eyes. 'OK, water break,' she said. 'It does makes your brain work better,' she added.

'What do you mean, it makes my brain work better?' I said tensely. Superbrain or not, I wasn't going to sit there and let her ridicule me!

'It makes *everyone's* brain work better,' Steph said slowly, interrupting my internal rant. 'It's basic biology.'

I nodded, feeling a little embarrassed as Naomie left the room. I'm anything but sensitive, right? OK, maybe I was a little sensitive about my brain right then because it *didn't* seem to be working. The way the lines seeped out like water through a sieve, the way they sometimes got stuck and then came apart, then got back together in the wrong order. I'd never noticed it much before, but I did now, and although I realized I had to do something about it, I knew my problem was not going to be solved here, however hard Naomie or Steph tried.

*

I'll spare you the long and tedious details of how the next hour went, but let's just say I wasn't wrong. Neither the genius Naomie, the future teacher Steph nor Jaz the bookworm were able to do much for me, although they did their very best to help.

Steph would read my lines, and I would say them wrong, then she'd go over them again and again and AGAIN. Then Jaz would explain what she thought a scene was about and would go off on a tangent about what part of the book it was drawn from. I could tell from the look on Naomie's face that she didn't really understand why I just couldn't seem to get it. Neither did I. One teeny-tiny step forward and a zillion huge strides back!

19

Summer Steals the Show

'Kind of you to join us, Charligh,' Dodson said as I arrived at the lunchtime rehearsal, having lost track of time in the girls' toilet making sure my quiff was perfect.

'Thanks,' I replied, unsure whether he was being sarcastic or not.

As a drama teacher, you'd think he'd be capable of stronger facial expressions. I considered sharing that piece of friendly advice – you know, actor to actor – but seeing the frosty look behind his glasses I decided to save any tips for another time.

The second thing that hit me upon entering our rehearsal session was that everyone was gathered on the stage, crowded round Summer ... who was singing MY finale song!! It was 'A Million Annes' to the tune of Luther Vandross's 'Never Too Much'. The cheek!

Not so fast, Summer.

I strode up the steps to the stage in two quick strides. Well, it would have been two quick strides had I not stumbled on the second step, whacked my chin and ended up on my hands and knees. *Ugh*.

Between you and me, though, the worst blow was to my pride, which had certainly taken a knock.

I stood up, wiping the grit of the assembly hall floor from my hands and chin, and as I did so I could see that the situation was worse – much worse – than I'd thought. Dodson hadn't even seen me fall – he was too busy smiling at the gaggle of pupils who stood around, looking enraptured as Summer gave a rendition of MY SONG.

It was horrible, like soul-crushingly, world-stoppingly, universe-rockingly horrid in EPIC proportions. Why was she trying to ruin my life? This was my stage, my song and my turn to shine. It wasn't Reception class any more – things had changed. She just had to accept it: I was the main character while her role was that of a supporting actor. *Anne and Friends* was my show!

'Stop!' I said firmly from behind her, using my Assertive Voice. If she thought me being ten minutes late gave her licence to steal the spotlight right out from under my size two feet, she had another think coming.

It seemed nobody heard me, except for Summer, of course, because she smiled right at me as she filled the last verse with runs and riffs and held that last note perhaps a split second longer than I ever would. When she finally did stop, the relief I felt was drowned out by EVERYONE's applause.

I stared at the tiny beauty spot on the tip of Summer's nose, wishing hard it would explode and become a great big dark hole to swallow her up until the play was over.

'Now could everyone please sit round in a circle. Before we launch into today's rehearsal, Summer has been working on something very special that she'll be sharing and also teaching us today,' said Dodson after we'd done some vocal warm-ups. 'I'll let her explain.'

Summer stepped into the middle, a pleased smile on her face . 'As some of you know –' she paused – 'OK, well, as *everyone* knows . . . Erica, Rosie and I are basically Bramrock's TikTok queens, and we do tons of dance challenges online that get a lot of views, and thousands of other kids follow us.'

I rolled my eyes, wishing she'd just get to the point, because the school production was, like, a zillion miles away from the VIP's TikTok channel.

'Well, I have – with the help of my friends – choreographed a dance for the final song "A Million Annes". And I'll be teaching you all the entire routine today. It's very simple. Anyone can do it,' she said breezily, looking me dead in the eye.

My heart sank. I'd seen the kind of dances the VIPs put online. They were like a web of complicated steps and moves that I couldn't keep up with, even if I'd wanted to, which I didn't. I could act, I could sing and I could dance – sort of. But now I was being asked to do all of those things at once, and I knew it was just going to be too much.

By the end of practice, I had proved myself right. I kept speaking at the wrong part, or when it was actually my turn, I'd either recite my lines perfectly from the wrong scene, or *kind of* remember the correct lines, but get my words muddled up.

I just didn't understand it. I'd always been a performer, born for the stage – everyone said it – so why was I getting stuck now? It couldn't be stage fright. I didn't feel any kind of nervousness at all. But when it was my turn to recite lines, everything I'd learned evacuated my brain totally at my moment of need. Instead, I was noticing everything I didn't need to notice: how Summer had one stray curl that would pop out of her otherwise straight hair, how Theo had a tiny gap in his left eyebrow, how Neeta kept sniffling loudly because of her allergies. And Summer's 'simple' dance steps were, as I'd suspected, completely NOT simple, and my moves just looked weird and awkward.

I couldn't help but begin to worry. There was nothing wrong with my brain . . . was there?

As we all got ready to leave the rehearsal, Dodson looked how I felt: frustrated and tired.

'OK, we've not got long until the dress rehearsal so it would be great if we could all learn our lines before then. Especially the leads. In fact, Charligh – could I have a word?'

My heart sank even further.

As everyone else began to file out of the hall, Dodson took me aside. 'Look, Charligh, as I've just said, it's not long until the first of our two dress rehearsals, and then one week until the final play. Now only you know how much effort you've put into learning your lines.'

He gave me a pointed look that clearly said he didn't think I'd made any effort at all.

'You only have one shot at this on the night, so use your practice time wisely – don't be afraid to fail, or to make mistakes, but you've got to try. I've never threatened to remove anyone from a play before.'

Dodson paused, looking thoughtful, and I thought my heart might stop.

'And I'm not going to now,' he continued. *Phew!*

'But I want you to remember how hard the whole cast has worked on this, and, if you don't think you can do the same, consider if it's really fair to your classmates to just try and wing it.'

'But I AM trying!' I said.

He raised his eyebrows high above his glasses. 'Really? You did appear to be making progress for a while, but lately it seems you've slacked off a bit – and sometimes we're back to square one. I believe you can do this – but you need to be more consistent. And, perhaps, dedicated.'

I wanted to tell Dodson that there's nothing I'm more dedicated to than performing onstage, and that I think about it ALL the time. I'd tried rehearsing by myself, tried with others – I'd even taken my script to the football residential course! But it was no wonder I hadn't practised as much as I should have lately. Failure was utterly demoralizing.

I bit my lip. If I told him all that, and he knew how much I was really struggling, maybe he would think I was just hopeless, and that Miss Williams had totally fluffed it with the casting.

Dodson looked a bit impatient now. 'Hello? Charligh?'

'OK, I'll try harder,' I said, feeling defeated.

What if this was my best ...? How could I ever be in the West End if I couldn't even learn the lines for my first school play?

'I'm glad to hear it. And one more thing. I'd like to set some ongoing homework for you. Anne Shirley's story is at the heart of this play, and everything hinges on Anne and her character arc. We've spoken in previous rehearsals about some of the key scenes and points in her journey. So I want you to reflect on her biggest "aha" moment. You know, the bit where she snaps her fingers and learns a lesson that changes her from the inside out. Think about what that lesson is.' Dodson smiled. 'It's of the utmost importance to the success of the play that everyone, but especially you, really "gets" their character.'

I nodded silently, wishing Dodson already had confidence that I knew my character inside and out. The act of impressing him was starting to feel like an insurmountable task. It was as if I'd made a few steps up the hill, then fallen back down to the bottom. The bell rang, and my cheeks burned as I hurried out of the hall. I was sure that to Summer and everyone else it was like watching a really hilarious disaster movie every single time I got up onstage now. Except it wasn't a movie, and it wasn't hilarious, because this was my real life, and I was the disaster and, really and truly, it felt like my acting career was over before it had even begun. I had started off the term as a budding star. Now I was a complete laughing stock.

20

An Invitation

Tuesday night's football practice was cancelled. Rhiannon and Miss Williams had decided it was too much of a risk to train on the semi-frozen pitch. A few of us Dreamers decided to go to Flora House instead. Jaz was having a FIFA video games evening with her dad, Steph was making pancakes with her little brothers, and Naomie was going bowling with her family. So it was just me, Talia, Allie and Layla. I was looking forward to seeing Not-Granny. (I now called Betty Not-Granny because a couple of the residents had asked if I was her granddaughter, so I'd told them she was Not-Granny, and then it sort of stuck, and I liked the name. She wasn't my granny, but having Granny in the name I called her felt nice.)

She had to have some magic words or pearls of wisdom for me that could make this forgetting-lines THING just disappear!

While Talia was playing chess with a woman called Joyce, and Layla was painting the nails of some of the others, I decided to go into the garden. Allie was learning to crochet with a few residents.

I twirled round on the patio, blowing into my hands to keep warm at the same time. It was so pretty; the red camellias, white winter honeysuckle and purple pansies lit up the rock garden. The frost covering the flowers, grass and even the benches made everything sparkle.

I dug my hands deep into my pockets and walked on to the crunchy grass, watching the white cloud my breath made dissipate in the cold air. I spun round in alarm as I heard tapping on the windowpane. It was Not-Granny wearing a thick faux-fur shawl.

She opened the door a crack. 'If you think I'm going out there for my old bones to freeze, you're very much mistaken, young Charligh.'

'It's far too cold, Not-Granny,' I said, 'but apart from that, don't you just love winter? There's something so moody and dramatic about it. Although I do love spring, summer and autumn as well,' I added thoughtfully.

Not-Granny nodded. 'Before it became a bit painful for my joints, I used to love the cold and winter. I enjoyed hot humid summers as much as I liked chilly dark winters. Seasons come and go, and there's a time for every season! The important thing is to enjoy it when it comes, but right now I suggest you come back in, and I'll make you a cuppa.'

Not-Granny made us both a mug of what looked like golden tea, and we sat down near Talia's chess game.

'This is the most delicious hot drink ever,' I gasped.

'I agree! It's turmeric, honey, black tea and ginger mixed with almond milk. They say it's a great boost for the immune system. I can't take credit for the recipe, though. I discovered it when we travelled to Mumbai on one of our tours.'

'Students from Sweden, Sri Lanka and even Canada have stayed at Meaden Lodge. They've had people from all over the world,' I said, thinking of the huge map and all the different locations marked with silver drawing pins.

'That sounds like a great place. One of the best things about travelling is getting to meet other people and encountering new cultures. I always say the people in a place are actually far more important than the place itself, no matter how grand or exotic it might seem. The touring life isn't for everyone, but I did so love it. We were like one big, happily mismatched family, whether we were hurrying through the winding streets of Las Ramblas in Barcelona, driving down the wide highways of LA, walking along a beach in Malaysia or a night market in Thailand. Taking unfamiliar roads and exploring new places can be challenging, but it doesn't have to be frightening.'

She paused, her eyes soft with memories as she sipped her Golden Tea. I wondered if I'd ever have the opportunity to experience the things she had. I'd always thought doing sell-out world tours would be a breeze, but now I wasn't so sure.

'Penny for your thoughts?' Not-Granny said, breaking the silence.

'A penny for my thoughts?' I said indignantly. 'More like a million bucks!'

Not-Granny laughed, then looked behind me, her face taking on a serious expression.

I turned round and saw that the chessboard in front of Talia was upside down, and Joyce appeared flustered, spinning in circles and running her hands through her hair. 'You're not my Ashley,' she was mumbling over and over again.

Nari and another carer were over in a flash, soothing Joyce in steady tones and leading her over to the lift while Allie and Talia picked up the chess pieces.

'Dementia?' I asked quietly.

Not-Granny nodded, looking sad. 'Joyce is one of the younger residents too. It's never nice for the dementia sufferer or for those witnessing it, but luckily her son and daughter are coming to visit tomorrow. Dementia is very sad and difficult . . .' Her voice drifted off as we watched Joyce get into the lift, then she smiled again. 'Anyway, how's your play going?' she said.

'*Mmm* . . .' I picked at a bit of chipped nail polish. 'OK,' I mumbled unhappily as I imagined LOCAL STAR PUPIL LETS DOWN HER FANS plastered across the front of the national newspapers.

Not-Granny looked at me shrewdly. 'I'm assuming it's not going quite as smoothly as you planned. Well, whatever the case may be, I have full confidence that you'll be ready for opening night. You're a brilliant performer.'

'Not any more. I'm trying so hard, but no one can see it. Instead, Dodson keeps going on about dedication and commitment as if acting isn't the only thing I've ever wanted to do,' I said, folding my arms.

Not-Granny smiled softly. 'Ah, but wanting to do something is never enough, Charligh, even if you have bags of talent, which I know you do. To become a great actor, you need passion, perseverance and practice! If you're missing any of these, things start to get out of balance. Don't just wait for inspiration to strike before you sit down and learn your lines. You need to find your own way to do it consistently. Remember: what might work for others won't necessarily work for you.'

She was right, but at the same time I felt like I'd tried everything, and nothing I did seemed to make the lines really stick in my mind. I wanted to believe I could still find the route to success, but I was just as lost now as when I was orienteering in the New Forest.

'Well, anyway,' Not-Granny continued kindly, 'speaking of plays, I have a surprise for you and your friends. One of my old students, Arielle Starr, is the casting producer for *Cats* in the West End, and they're coming to the Theatre Royal Brighton. I told her all about the Dreamers, especially you, Charligh, and asked if I could have a few more spare tickets, and she said yes. Not only that, but she's invited us all backstage. Would you like to come?'

'Would I like to come? Would I like to come?!' I repeated incredulously. 'Yes. Yes, yes!'

I ran off to round up Talia, Allie and Layla, and together we FaceTimed the rest of the Fabulous Four. I got Not-Granny in the call to invite all the Dreamers to *Cats*, and everyone squealed with excitement and said yes, they'd like that very much.

That evening I almost – but not quite – forgot the impending doom of the play, which was drawing nearer. My face felt like it would split from smiling so hard! Not only were we going to see *Cats*, but we'd been invited backstage too!

I may not have learned my own lines for the play, but rubbing shoulders with real-life West End actors was just up my street!

21

Superspies

Some say it's espionage, many call it subterfuge, others may even describe it as *reconnaissance*, but today I called it ... Operation Silverstone! And this is why we were at the sports ground of our not-so-beloved rivals, the Silverstone Shiners, at 10 a.m. on Sunday watching them play against Mertonville FC. Both teams were high up in the league. They were the ones we needed to beat – the two squads that most threatened our chances of winning.

I tilted my beige fedora and slipped on my

wide square sunglasses. We had to take out the enemy, and being here, finding out more about their game and hopefully taking advantage of their weaknesses, was just what we needed to do to secure another Dreamer win.

Jaz was wearing her brother Jordan's mustard cap, camouflage leggings and a brown, oversized hoodie.

I gave her a mock salute. 'Atten-*shun*!' I shouted.

'Shh . . . or you'll blow our cover before we even get started. And I don't know what you're teasing me for. This "mission" was all your idea, and you said to dress in camouflage,' Jaz said in defence of her fashion fail.

'No one will suspect a thing,' I said reassuringly.

Of course, after having advised Jaz to wear camouflage, I realized I didn't have anything myself, so I'd simply gone for an understated look: a stone-coloured coat that had puffy sleeves and flared out at the bottom like a cape, topped off by my fedora.

The only thing working against us was that the weather forecast had been completely wrong. Although the sky was grey, it was a lot warmer than it'd told us it would be, so not only were we both burning up, but my heavy coat and Jaz's hoodie were making us stand out rather than blend in.

'Oh no, don't look now, but Beehive is coming,' Jaz hissed.

Beehive, whose real name is Mrs Chatton, was the mother of Victoria, one of the best Shiner players, and she had a VICIOUS habit of tearing down the opposition in casual – not-so-friendly – pre-game chats.

I spun round and saw Mrs Chatton striding towards us.

'I said, don't look!' Jaz groaned.

I laid a hand on her shoulder. 'Don't panic – just follow my lead,' I said bravely. 'As long as we act like we're not spies on a mission, we're not spies on a mission, and therefore won't attract any attention.'

Beehive marched past us without a second glance.

Jaz exhaled loudly. 'I can't believe I let you talk me into this.'

'See! She didn't recognize us at all,' I said triumphantly as we watched Jilly Hutchinson, the Shiners' captain and their star striker, zigzag her way through the defenders in the opposition box and fire their first goal in just before half-time.

They definitely haven't lost their touch. If anything, they're even better, I thought.

'They're so good,' Jaz said, biting her lip anxiously.

I was hoping Operation Silverstone would cheer her up when she saw we had nothing to worry about, but it was having the opposite effect.

'Hey, let's go and get something to drink,' I said, spotting a food kiosk. 'Half-time's coming up and holding a hot chocolate will make us look even less like spies.'

'Who are we supposed to be again?' Jaz asked as we walked over to the kiosk.

'Assistant junior youth coaches, helping our bosses scout for talent to see who wants to join the new eleven-a-side team in September,' I said.

'*Riiiiight*,' Jaz replied doubtfully.

'Two mint chocolate frappuccinos, with whipped cream and chocolate chips, please,' I said to the teenage girl behind the counter.

'That'll be four pounds eighty.' She held out her hand, which had very long and very pink nails with tiny gems on the tips. I loved them!

'My treat,' I said as Jaz started to dig around in her pockets.

'Are you sure?'

'Absolutely. It was my idea.' I opened my purse and counted out the money.

We grabbed our drinks when they were ready, but, as I swung round, somehow I'd forgotten to zip up my purse, and all the coins flew out. I immediately bent down to pick them up, and that's when I realized I'd forgotten I was holding my drink, and a lot of it had spilled on the ground.

'Please be careful, young lady,' I heard a familiar shrill voice say.

I looked up gingerly at Mrs Chatton, who was wiping splatters of frappuccino off her cream boots and tutting in annoyance.

I stood up sharply and somehow managed to headbutt Jaz, who was bending down to help me pick up my money.

'Ow!' She clutched her forehead, knocking her cap off, which went flying in the wind over to the pitch, just as the whistle blew for half-time.

'Hood – pull your hood up,' I hissed.

'You two look familiar,' Mrs Chatton said, coming closer and eyeing both of us intently.

'We're youth coaches,' Jaz said.

'Is it just me or do they look a bit young?' Mrs Chatton said sharply to Kiosk Girl, who just shrugged and started wiping down the counter.

'We are *assistants* to youth coaches,' I said in my most grown-up voice.

'Junior assistants, so we're … erm … going round scouting to see if any girls want to join our eleven-a-side team,' Jaz added weakly.

Mrs Chatton suddenly looked terribly excited. 'That sounds wonderful! Are there any sponsors for your team?'

'Um, what?' said Jaz.

'Yes, sponsors, lots of sponsors,' I said. 'We're running out of room for our sponsors. We're simply oozing sponsors.'

'I recommend you focus on number seven,' said Beehive. 'From the Silverstones. She's extremely good and open to joining a new team,' she added in a hushed tone. 'You know what?' She squinted at the pitch. 'It's half-time, so why don't you wander over and speak to her? You'll see what a great asset she'd be to your team.'

There was a look of panic in Jaz's eyes. I knew what she was thinking, and she was right. We may have just about managed to fool Mrs Chatton, but any one of the Shiners would recognize us instantly. Especially Jilly, who was basically Jaz's mortal enemy on the pitch.

I had to think on my feet and fast!

'We just need to consult some notes, and we'll be right over. No need to wait for us.' I pulled out my phone and concentrated hard on the screen, muttering and making 'thinking' sounds every few seconds.

Mrs Chatton seemed to get the hint and started moving away, probably to tell her daughter about us.

'*Ruuuun!*' I said to Jaz as I swigged what was left of my frappuccino and threw the paper cup in the recycling bin.

We didn't look back or stop for a rest until we got round the corner. Then we both collapsed on a wooden bench outside the sports building, laughing.

I tugged at my football laces and wiggled my left foot. A few seconds earlier, my boot had gone flying when I'd kicked a ball, only narrowly missing Naomie's head. Good thing Layla had collected the ball on the left wing and was now dribbling her way through the Rosewell Thorns Community Youth defence. As I turned my attention to my right shoe, I felt a soft whoosh of air as something went flying by my ear. I untied and retied my laces, tightening them. *There!* I thought, feeling satisfied.

I noticed that Naomie, Steph – in fact, everyone – seemed to be making their way down to our end, and Layla no longer had the ball. The ball! That was what had whizzed by me – oops!

I spun round and, to my huge relief, Allie was cradling the ball protectively. She must have saved it, so we were still 1–0 up.

'Keep your eye on the ball,' Allie said after she'd rolled it up to Naomie, who kicked it on to Steph in the centre.

'It was an emergency, Allie,' I said. 'Do you or do you not want my boot to knock someone out the next time I take a kick?'

Naomie quickly intervened. 'Allie, it's done now, and Charligh did need to stop her shoe from going flying again. Great save, though! Charligh, maybe you should look into Velcro boots,' Naomie added. 'My sister also hates laces, so it's Velcro shoes all the way for her!'

Allie sniggered as Naomie moved back to her position. Naomie hadn't meant it maliciously, but I was a TAD irritated by Allie being so tickled at the suggestion of me needing the same shoes as Naomie's little sister, which, of course, I didn't.

Fives minutes later, the whistle blew, and we cheered at our victory against the Thorns.

'Another win,' said Layla as she pulled me in for a hug.

No *thanks to me*, I thought, still feeling ashamed at how I'd nearly let a goal in.

I forced a smile as Rhiannon and Miss Williams gathered us together for our usual post-match huddle.

'Great match, girls,' said Miss Williams enthusiastically. 'This is our third win in a row.

We have some of our more difficult team challenges ahead, but let's not worry about the opposition.'

'Right,' said Jaz. 'We're going to concentrate on ourselves and what WE can do.' She exchanged a look with Rhiannon.

Rhiannon gave her a nod. 'So, I've been thinking. We need to get more on the attack, so I've decided it's time to move on from our two-two-two formation and consider looking at one-three-two. This means there will be one back – I think we'll try Naomie there – and then three midfielders and two strikers/forwards.'

My heart sank. More changes. I'd only just got used to playing defence.

Rhiannon said we'd try the new positions out a couple of times before the final fixture on March the twenty-second.

'That's the weekend before the play!' said Steph.

All of a sudden, I felt more nervous than I'd ever been before. Football, the play, Flora House, even the class presentation – everything that felt fun, all the things I loved the most, were suddenly piling up. And it didn't feel good.

Dear Charligh,

Huge greetings from everyone at Flora
House. We all miss you. Some of the other
girls have been to visit — your friend
Talia even taught me to play chess, and
she didn't let me win, which I think is
marvellous. She beat me in three straight
games!

I hope you're all looking forward to seeing
Cats next week. The whole cast is excited
about meeting the Dreamers. I'll be coming
along with Nari, who loves a good musical
too. We'll all gather in the foyer at 7 p.m.,
and I'd be delighted to meet the lovely
people who have raised such a brilliant
group of young ladies. I hope you're making
progress in learning your lines, and
remember — we each have our journey.
Find your way!

Yours sincerely,

Not-Granny

22

A Different Way of Thinking

The play is eleven days, three hours and thirty-seven minutes away, I thought as I got home from school on Monday. This week I would work hard at learning my part, but I wasn't super hopeful about the result. Nothing was quite going in, no matter how much I stared at the sharp black letters on the bright white paper. Well, it was white when I'd first got it. Now it was tea-stained and strawberry-jam-stained, so it was kind of a blend of off-white and multicoloured ...

Anyway, the issue was I was no closer to knowing my lines.

Is it possible to go backwards in how much you know? I wondered.

I looked it up in my online thesaurus and found the perfect word for it: regression. *Noun: to go backwards*. My performance skills were in regression. This play was *supposed* to help propel me to stardom, but instead I was further away from it than when I'd started.

Is that what a lot of Flora House residents were doing – regressing? It must be so hard to reach old age and have fine grey hair that makes you look really wise, but then struggle to do the things you'd always been able to do since you were the same age as the Tinies.

I frowned. I was only ten – nearly eleven, to be fair, but not THAT old. It wasn't dementia – I was sure of that. And, while I worried about what was wrong with me, the first dress rehearsal was slowly approaching, day by day, like a pirate urging me to walk the plank. It looked like the Very Worst Thing was going to happen.

I sighed and looked at my watch. There was just enough time to record another instalment of the *Charligh Green Show*. This time, I'd talk all about how my acting career was under threat. But, before I could begin, Mum called me down for dinner. Drat!

'Are you OK?' Mum asked after we'd eaten. Dad was putting the Tinies to bed, and she was loading the dishwasher. 'You've been spending a lot of time in your room this week.'

'*Hmm*, sort of. Well . . . to be honest, I still haven't learned all my lines,' I confessed. 'And every time I read through the play I start feeling more and more stressed. I haven't managed to read the book either.'

Mum looked thoughtful. 'I'm sorry to hear that, sweetheart. Maybe you could try connecting with the story in a different way? Why don't you watch a film adaptation of *Anne of Green Gables*?'

'Mum, you're a genius!' I jumped up and hugged her. Now why hadn't I thought of that earlier?

'I know. Now let's see if we can find *Anne* on the TV. Do you want to invite Jaz round?'

'Yes and yes,' I said, jumping up to find my phone.

The film was good. In fact, it was better than good – it was magnificent! I loved Anne Shirley the minute she appeared on the screen, and I finally saw her in a way I hadn't really got from the script. She was the most colourful character I'd ever seen! Anne was so confident and full of dreams, but she also worried a lot about what other people thought of her. Her imagination made her think silly thoughts like, *What if this person doesn't like me?* She was a talented poet and desperate to impress her teacher, but she learned that poetry was more than just using the frilliest, biggest words available. We were both wordsmiths, except I used my words on the stage or in front of a camera, whereas she crafted hers into poetry and put them down on paper. We were SO alike!

'I still think the book is better than the film,' announced Jaz at the end.

'Bookworms like you always say that. Personally, I don't think you can get better than this,' I said stubbornly, knowing that I couldn't really say one way or the other since I hadn't read the book.

'Now do you see why I said Anne is your kindred spirit?' Jaz said, grinning.

We did have a lot in common. Imagine if she was real! We would definitely be besties!

I remembered how Dodson gave me my own special assignment – to really get to the heart of my character's story. To figure out the big 'aha' moment of our journey. To be honest, I hadn't entirely understood what he was asking at the time, I was too busy being embarrassed at Summer upstaging me, but now I had it. I knew what Anne's journey was all about – learning to celebrate and accept her authentic self. She basically learns how to be herself instead of trying to impress others. Anne Shirley was fast turning into my new hero!

I always knew that Thursday was going to be a bit of a weird day because we had our appointment with the educational psychologist lady. Mum had reminded me about this last week but, between everything that had been happening with the play, football and Not-Granny, I'd forgotten all about it.

Mum had reminded me that morning, and I'd been given permission to leave the last class early – which definitely made up for any nerves I might have been feeling. It was maths too, so I had a bounce in my step as I skipped through the hallway towards the Learning Retreat, which was next to Mrs Forrest's office.

I hadn't been all that keen until Mum said both she and Miss Williams thought this might help with the trouble I was having learning my lines. Would the educational psychologist give me a special pill? Was she going to hypnotize me? My mind was quite dizzy with all the possibilities.

The Learning Retreat had plain white walls and a soft grey shaggy rug that pupils sometimes read or did puzzles on. My parents sat on either side of me as the educational psychologist, a young woman with copper-gold bobbed hair, introduced herself and shook our hands.

'So you must be Charligh, and Mr and Mrs Gorley. I'm Doctor Lincoln.'

Her accent had a twang to it. I knew that one – I'd been studying it since I'd first heard where the play was set.

'Canadian,' I announced triumphantly.

Dr Lincoln smiled. 'Good guess! You have a great ear for accents. Yes, I'm Canadian. Well, more specifically, I'm from one of the major cities in Canada called Montreal. It's a wonderful place, especially if you like cold winters. The whole city snuggles under a blanket of the coldest, whitest snow for about three months.'

'I hate the cold, but everything does look magical when it's covered in snow. Even Bramrock. I haven't had the chance to go to Canada, but I've been trying to learn the accent as I'm playing Anne Shirley in our school play. I take my role extremely seriously,' I added, hoping that this all sounded exceedingly grand and impressive.

She nodded. 'Yes, I've heard a little about that from Miss Williams. I'd love to find out more a bit later, but first let's go through some tests. And don't panic – you can't fail this assessment. The reason you're here today, Charligh, is because an initial screening indicated you might have a specific learning difference.'

I frowned. Mum had said this was just to help me understand more about how I learn things – so I could memorize my lines – not to tell me I had something wrong with me.

'There's no need to look so worried,' Dr Lincoln said kindly. 'A specific learning difference just means a different way of learning and thinking. Shall we begin?'

She gave me a variety of tests to do. Some tested my vocabulary (I think I did really well in those!), another was a mental arithmetic test (I don't think I did quite so well there), and there were various puzzles, patterns and sequences for me to figure out. There was also a general-knowledge quiz – that was fun, but I thought I'd know more of the answers than I did. I suppose, when it's not to do with musicals, vintage movies or football, I don't know quite as much.

Sometimes Dr Lincoln asked me questions and recorded the answers, but for some of them, like the block-design test or visual puzzles, I could just work through them myself. She also asked my parents questions, like when did I say my first words? What age was I when I crawled, walked, sat up? How long had it taken me to ride a bike?

This last question was put to all three of us.

'I got stabilizers at the start of Year Two, but it wasn't until I was in Year Three,' I said. 'I remember my stabilizers being removed the night before my eighth birthday.'

'That's right,' said Mum. 'It took you nearly two years, and you were so determined!'

Dr Lincoln smiled. 'I'm getting a picture of a very determined young person. What about other sports? I hear that you play for a football team. What are your strengths – do you think you dribble quite well?'

'I'm . . . OK,' I mumbled, wondering why she'd picked the one thing I'm completely useless at.

'She trips over the ball a lot,' Dad said.

Thanks, Dad.

'How about swimming?' Dr Lincoln asked.

I felt myself blushing. 'Well, I'm still learning to swim.'

It was like someone was shining a light on all the things I couldn't do but was supposed to. And I already knew I was no good at that stuff, so what was the point in going over it again here? I just wanted help with learning lines.

Then she asked us other questions about the SATs, and juggling all my after-school activities with schoolwork. I hadn't thought much about that before, but I suppose I'd mostly been muddling through. Some subjects were harder than others, whether it was geography where I could never colour inside the lines of those maps, or maths problems that I could never solve, but without fail my homework was always done at the last minute. And I wasn't sure how much I was able to remember from all my lessons.

Finally, Dr Lincoln took off her glasses, put her papers aside and said, 'I'll be writing a full report, but I wanted to say upfront that I think Charligh presents as having dyspraxia.'

Mum nodded, like she understood, and Dad looked thoughtful. It seemed it was only me who didn't have a clue what she was talking about.

'What's that?'

'About two to ten per cent of people have some degree of dyspraxia. It's a form of what's called neurodivergence. So it falls under the same umbrella of conditions such as dyslexia, dysgraphia and dyscalculia. Your specific set of symptoms would suggest dyspraxia, which is a specific learning difference, known as SpLD for short. It affects coordination, spatial awareness and sensory processing. I'll explain a bit more in the report exactly what that means for you, Charligh, and how it impacts your learning – including memorizing lines. But you should know it's very common for dyspraxic people to struggle with time management and short-term memory.'

'You said it impacts sensory processing – I wonder . . . are dyspraxic children more likely to be put off by certain foods?' Dad asked, sheepishly.

'Yes! And very often dyspraxic children are unfairly labelled as fussy eaters,' said Dr Lincoln.

I think Dad was feeling bad for calling me a fussy eater and not really believing me when I said the material of some of my clothes made me itch.

'I have students who have learning differences. I'm just surprised I never spotted it in Charligh,' Mum said, looking a bit guilty.

Oh no, now Mum's feeling bad too.

'Don't worry. The presence of these things on their own does not necessarily suggest an SpLD, so it's understandable how difficult it is to detect. Children – and adults – with dyspraxia often overcompensate. They find creative ways to get round the things they struggle with. But this can take its toll if they're expending a lot more energy keeping up.'

Mum relaxed a bit. 'So Charligh being diagnosed relatively early means we can look at helping her access the support she needs quickly.'

'Definitely. Some things might take a little while to change, but, once Charligh understands the methods that work for her, things will really improve,' said Dr Lincoln. She waved her papers at us. 'And Miss Williams will be helping in discussions to set up an IEP, which is an individual education plan. Charligh is a very able student in many areas of the curriculum, and her scores show that, despite her reluctance to read books, she has gained much in creative intelligence, vocabulary and general literacy through the other art forms she enjoys.'

I'd never thought of my ability to do improv, put on different accents and think of a backstory for the characters I make up as creative intelligence, but I suppose there are different types of smartness. Some are more obvious, such as being gifted in STEM like Naomie, or having an endless knowledge of plants, animals and nature like Steph, but there's also Layla's intelligence in writing heartfelt poems, or Allie's cleverness in using her hands to do things like crocheting.

'Any questions, Charligh?' Mum said.

I shook my head. Actually, I had loads, but I was still trying to take everything in.

Dr Lincoln gathered all her papers and folders and stood up. 'I wish you all the best in your acting career, Charligh, and something tells me you have a glittering future ahead of you! I look forward to seeing you in the West End one day.'

'Thank you,' I said. 'I just hope I can learn my lines.'

'A key strength of dyspraxia is the ability to think a bit differently from most neurotypical – that is, non-neurodivergent – people. So maybe you'll have to think outside the box to learn your lines.'

'If there's one thing we can rely on Charligh to do, it's to think differently,' Dad said, smiling.

I grinned. I was still figuring out how I felt about being dyspraxic, but overall it seemed like a step in the right direction. I was going to get lots of help and support, which would make things easier for me, and Dr Lincoln said she believed I could still be an actor. I'd come here to find out how to learn my lines, but it looked like I was going to get heaps more help with everything now.

It's strange, because I'd always felt a bit different. Maybe even slightly awkward or weird, but now that I had an actual name for it, it actually made me feel less different, because I knew there was a whole bunch of other people with dyspraxia whose minds worked a bit more like mine. The Charligh Show WOULD go on!

23

Cats!

Dear Not-Granny,

I have some wonderful and rather life-changing news to tell you. An EP (that's what they call educational ~~psycologsts,~~ psychologists, by the way – I'm not sure if you had them when you were younger) gave me some tests and assessments.

Does that sound ~~complecated?~~ complicated? If it does, just wait till you hear what I'm going to tell you next – I have ~~dsypra~~ ~~dysprax~~ dyspraxia. Ugh, it's a real pain to spell! But on the bright

side it explains why my handwriting is messy, I
get my words muddled up, and why I'm so
clumsy on the pitch. But most of all, why I'm
having so much trouble doing stuff like learning
my lines! It's as if the wires in my head are a
bit jumbled up.

But one thing I won't forget is our trip to the
theatre this weekend. I've watched Cats a zillion
times, but I know nothing beats live theatre ...

See you on Saturday!

Love and drama,

Charligh Green xx

*

Mum, Dad and even the Tinies all cheered. I'd
done it – finally! I'd swum without any of my
flotation aids! I'd begun the swimming session
with only a float to help me, instead of the usual
armbands, and then a happy accident occurred –
one of the floats drifted away, and I went to grab
it. Without even really thinking about it, I swam to
get it back, and then I realized – I didn't need it any
more. I was swimming – not even doggy-paddle

but front crawl! I was reaching out one arm after the other like I'd been doing this forever.

'Like a duck takes to water,' Dad said with a huge grin that reached from ear to ear, holding a twin in each arm.

Mum had swum over and was hugging me. 'I knew you could do it, Charligh! I'm so proud of you!'

I tried to play it cool, like I wasn't that bothered, but, after all those years of wearing armbands and watching the babies swim, I was dancing inside. Yes! I could do this now!

It had been two days since I'd seen Dr Lincoln, and I wished I could tell her that I had finally learned to swim. Wasn't that one of the things she said was hard for a kid with dyspraxia to learn? It had taken me a little while to figure out exactly how I felt about my diagnosis, but I know now that the fact that it's harder for me to do some things that come easily to other people is something to be proud of. When I mastered a new skill, it means I've worked twice as hard as most people.

Mum gave me a proud smile.

'You must be so looking forward to seeing Not-Granny at *Cats* tonight. How kind of her to organize this treat for you all.'

I'm sure it will be a purr-fect night to remember!' Dad said.

'I can't wait either, but now it's time for the Gorley trio to swim.'

I put a flamingo-pink swimming ring round each of the twins and got on to a raft, balancing Rory and Reuben on either side, before plonking myself in the middle. 'We're imagining we're on a tropical island, OK, boys?'

They nodded in agreement as they copied me, holding still and trying to keep their balance.

Then finally, FINALLY, it was time to go and see *Cats*!!

The Dreamers were all gathered in the foyer of the Theatre Royal with Nari and Not-Granny. I looked at my hair in the reflection of one of the large mirrors on the wall. Mum had done my favourite hair style: the Curly Pompadour. That had involved a lot of hairspray, pins and backcombing so my hair stood up in a quiff while the sides were tucked back and the rest hung down in gentle waves.

I looked around. I'd been to the Theatre Royal twice before and loved the way it looked. The foyer had a wine-red carpet with a gold swirl design, and wide stairs with shiny brown banisters led to the upper floors. Ornate chandeliers hung from the ceiling.

Soon an usher came and led us to our seats in the stalls. We were split across two rows, so Jaz and I sat with Not-Granny between us, and Allie and Layla on our other sides. Directly behind us were Rhiannon, Nari, Naomie, Steph and Talia.

'Glad you could come along, Allie,' I said. I'd never have thought a musical would be her thing.

She screwed up her face as if she didn't believe I was being serious.

I held up my hands. 'Honest, Allie. I'm really glad you came. And you look really nice.'

I noticed this was one of the first times outside school that I'd seen her in anything other than a tracksuit. Her nutmeg corkscrew curls, which were usually held back in a low ponytail, bounced out round her head.

She had even presented Not-Granny with an early birthday gift in the foyer – a crocheted honey-yellow scarf she'd made.

I hadn't known it was Not-Granny's birthday that soon. 'What are you planning for your birthday?' I asked her now.

'Nothing this year. It gets a bit repetitive when you've celebrated it nearly ninety times before,' Not-Granny said, chuckling.

'Not even a teeny-tiny surprise party?' I put my hand over my mouth.

'You're not supposed to ask people if they want a surprise party,' said Talia disapprovingly.

Not-Granny smiled. 'Don't worry, girls. I've had more than enough surprise parties in my day. Let's just call this an early birthday celebration for me – a night out at the theatre, in the best seats in the house and backstage access, with the best girls' football team in Bramrock.'

I clutched Not-Granny's arm. 'I can't wait to go backstage! It will be THEEEE most exciting thing EVER!'

'You say that about a lot of stuff,' said Jaz, giggling.

'Shh,' said Nari. 'The show's about to start!'

People scrambled to take their seats as the lights dimmed and the curtains began to draw back.

The orchestra played the musical's dramatic overture, and then the cast sprang on to the stage! Normally, when I'm at home watching this opening number, I sing along, clap, maybe even dance too, but right then I was rooted to my seat, and I didn't want to utter a single word.

'It's even better than watching the film,' I whispered to no one in particular.

The musical moved on to the naming of the cats. That was then followed by Rum Tum Tugger's song – he's the cat who oozes effortless confidence and coolness and has the most soulful voice and rhythmic movements. I loved how he was singing about himself and all the fans that flock to him.

Before we knew it, it was the interval between Acts 1 and 2, and I bought a butterscotch ice cream. I opened the *Cats* programme while Jaz was in the toilets and Not-Granny was talking to Layla. I discovered that *Cats* actually comes from a book called *Old Possum's Book of Practical Cats* by T. S. Eliot, and Andrew Lloyd Webber set the verses to music. One of my favourite songs in the second act is 'Memory', based on T. S. Eliot's unpublished poem 'Grizabella the Glamour Cat'.

As the familiar melody played, I thought how heart-wrenching and beautiful it was, as Grizabella, dressed in greyish white garments, sang in sombre, sad tones about memories of days gone by.

At the end, when all the actors came back onstage for a final encore, I screamed especially loudly for Rum Tum Tugger, Mr Mistoffelees and also for Grizabella as my heart just broke for her.

'That was marvellous,' I said, wide-eyed, to Not-Granny as we all began to stand up ready to exit the theatre.

'It was iconic,' declared Talia, to my absolute astonishment.

'It seems your enthusiasm is rubbing off on your friends,' Not-Granny said, trying not to laugh. 'Come on now, ladies, it's time to meet Arielle, who is the casting director for the masterpiece we have just witnessed tonight.'

Arielle, who was wearing a glitzy black top over black leather trousers, spent the first five minutes exclaiming how lucky we all were to know Not-Granny, who she called a 'stellar stalwart of the acting world'. Then she gave us a whistle-stop tour of the backstage dressing rooms and finally took us to the green room, where the actors where.

'It has been *utterly* wonderful to meet you all,' drawled Arielle. 'We have hordes of people lining up for the backstage meet-and-greet so the actors will be over any minute now to see you all before we open the door to the masses.' She wiped her forehead as if it was dripping sweat. 'While we're waiting, does anyone have any questions?'

My hand shot up.

'Sweetie, we're not in school here – although I do hope it's a learning experience. Just shout out your question, Charligh.'

'You remembered my name!' I said, feeling thrilled.

Arielle smiled. 'Being on the road, constantly meeting people and having to put names to faces, means you get quite good at that. What was your question?'

I looked down, suddenly nervous, doubting myself once more. 'How do you know if you have what it takes to be in the spotlight?'

Arielle smiled at me. 'I think, if you truly carry that ambition in your heart, and you want it badly enough, it's a mix of determination, daring and discipline. When I select my cast, I need to make sure they can *become* their role. It's not only who they are now, it's their potential to become someone else. And that, my dear, is the beauty of acting. Any other questions?' she said.

'I'm the stage manager of our school play, and I was wondering if you have any advice for making sure things run smoothly?' Steph said.

'Stage manager – an extremely important job. Actors are typically a dramatic lot so it's crucial for you to keep calm even when others aren't.' She smiled at someone behind us, and we all turned to see who it was. It was the cast!

'It's photo time, and if you want your programmes signed, don't be too shy to ask!' Not-Granny said.

Over the next five minutes, we took pictures with members of the cast and Arielle.

'I think I speak on behalf of all the cast when I say that we'd love to hear the legendary Betty Langton sing,' said Arielle, rather solemnly.

The cast murmured in agreement, and I began to see how much of a big deal Not-Granny really was in theatre circles, although she played it down for some reason.

'How about I do a duet with Charligh?' said Not-Granny. 'We all know "Circle of Life", don't we? Charligh and I will lead, and everyone else who knows the words can join in the chorus!'

It all happened so fast that I didn't really have enough time to be nervous, and, as Not-Granny began, I jumped in without a second thought for the fact that I was performing in front of some of the country's very best theatre professionals! The Dreamers and several of the cast joined in the chorus, and everyone applauded when it was over.

Peter, the actor who was playing Rum Tum Tugger, said he had no doubt that he'd be asking for my autograph soon if I carried on like this!

I was tingling all over long after we left the Theatre Royal. I know that acting isn't all frills and thrills and laughter. It is long evenings, hard slog and dedication, but it's worth it for moments like THIS. Every minute I wasn't playing football or at school, I'd be learning my lines and the choreography. I knew what I had to do to get to the place of my dreams!

24

A Dress Rehearsal

Butterflies fluttered in my stomach and hummed in my ears as we got ready for the first dress rehearsal. But I'm THRILLED to tell you I wasn't nervous, not really. I mean, I'd worked so incredibly hard to learn all my lines. *Aaaand* singing in the Theatre Royal with Not-Granny and the cast of *Cats* had been more than a little boost to my confidence, shall we say.

I'd certainly had my ups and downs over the past three months, but today, with just seven days to go until the final performance, I really felt like

I could do this. And wasn't half of acting matching how you felt on the inside to how you looked on the outside? Well, thanks to Not-Granny, all of us could now pass for bona fide stars.

We'd all gathered at the Bramrock Performance Hub for the dress rehearsal, and we were even allowed to get changed in proper actors' dressing rooms! But, best of all, Not-Granny had come to help with our hair and make-up. She was wearing a huge faux-fur jacket, and her silver-grey hair was in an elegant low bun with a wavy fringe at the front. Her skin was glowing, and I'd never seen her look more alive, not even when we went to see *Cats*.

'Did you really perform in the West End?' Summer asked Not-Granny, looking awed. She seemed thrilled to meet a real-life actor, and something almost resembling a smile was on her face.

'That's right, and on Broadway in New York too. I was fortunate enough that my childhood dream of being a theatre actor came true.'

I tightened the bows at the end of my two pigtails and smoothed out the invisible creases in my dress. I glanced over at Summer, who was now looking in the mirror and silently reciting her lines, and felt a bit intimidated. She looked so confident, like she'd done this before.

Not-Granny saw me looking and must have sensed that I was maybe a *little* bit nervous after all.

'I know you can do this. You have "star" written all over you. And remember, this is all part of the journey. Enjoy it!'

We'd done a mic check, the lighting was perfect and the stage design looked brilliant. Our background was lush green plants and bushes surrounding a lake, and a clear, wide blue sky. Miss Williams and some of our classmates had worked hard at it, and it looked amazing – I really felt as if I was on Prince Edward Island. Matthew's armchair at the Cuthberts' house was near the centre at the back of the stage. All of us were ready – or as ready as we were ever going to be.

I took a peek round the curtain. Our sole audience member – Not-Granny – was sitting in the front row, her handbag perched beside her.

I grinned. She really looked like she was here for a real musical.

And then, finally, it was time!

After Talia had finished her opening narration, I listened to Miss Williams playing the intro melody to 'Here Comes Anne', and tapped my hand on my leg softly to the beat – 1, 2, 3, 4, 1, 2, 3, 4 – as Naomie harmonized with her saxophone. Taking a deep breath, I joined in perfectly at the third bar. I could see by Dodson's and Not-Granny's facial expressions that I was hitting every note, and all my nerves simply melted away. I finished the song without a hitch, and relief and gratitude swelled up in me. My head felt clear and calm, and I was ready for the next scene. I picked up Anne's small brown leather suitcase and moved into position, ready to engulf Theo in hugs and happy tears.

'You're not what we were expecting,' said Theo shyly. He was all kitted out in his Matthew Cuthbert-style high-waisted brown trousers, white shirt, braces and a rather wonderful bowler hat.

There was a split-second pause that very gradually turned into one long, agonizing minute.

Oh no! I KNEW these lines, I know I did . . . I heard Summer cough loudly, and I could even hear the large white-faced clock tick-tock, tick-tock.

Then I saw Not-Granny's face. She looked hopeful, calm and patient. And I admired her lovely hairstyle again. Wait. That was it!

I touched my hair. 'Yes, they may not have told you quite how red my hair is or how skinny I am.'

'It's not that,' Theo said. 'We were expecting a boy.'

Before I could even think, I heard myself saying the next line: 'I'm whip-smart, hard-working and diligent. Just give me a chance and you'll be glad the orphanage made this mistake.'

Theo beamed, even though he wasn't actually supposed to be smiling, but I suppose, like me, he was just so happy that the lines finally seemed to have stuck! We sailed through the rest of Act 1 and then took a break in the middle of Act 2.

I had the type of exhilarating feeling you get when you realize that you've not failed the assignment. There were times when the rehearsal had been difficult – sometimes there were slight pauses and confusion – but when I really concentrated and focused, the lines came at just the right time. It was like I wasn't even saying them: they were just coming from somewhere deep inside my brain.

But then something horrible happened.

During the break, I was in the toilets, readjusting my dress, when I heard Erica and Amarachi come in, talking to Summer.

'She's so wooden! I just don't know why they gave her the lead role,' came Summer's Arctic tones.

'She has a really good voice,' Amarachi said. 'I can't think of anyone who can reach those high notes like she can . . .' Her voice trailed off. I could almost see Summer staring Amarachi down.

'But what about her ability to learn her lines? This isn't just about singing, is it?' Summer retorted frostily. 'And don't even get me started on the dancing! It's like she can't even follow the simple routine I've put together. Is she just not very clever, or is it stage fright?'

I winced as I flushed the toilet, drowning out the rest of Summer's poisonous words, and waited a few seconds as I heard Erica gasp. I swung the door out so hard it bounced against the wall. Then I put my head up and gave them all the biggest smile in the mirror as I walked out of the toilet cubicle and washed my hands at the sink furthest away from them.

Even Summer had the sense not to look at me as they all scurried out.

My shoulders immediately slumped once they'd gone and I had no one to pretend for. My lip trembled, but I blinked the tears away angrily, annoyed at the thought of ruining the make-up Not-Granny had applied. It's not as if I was bothered about Summer being mean. She didn't know how else to be. She'd probably had a MEAN GIRL chip implanted deep inside her the second she'd arrived on the delivery table in the Royal Sussex County Hospital maternity ward. But something other than her deeply programmed meanness had hit home.

I looked the part of Anne Shirley, and after watching the *Anne of Green Gables* film I knew what Anne felt like as a character. I'd even finally managed to learn my lines ... but now it appeared that my star quality had deserted me.

Just as I was glumly making my way along the corridor back to the hall, I bumped into Not-Granny.

'Just who I was looking for,' she said. I noticed her normally strong voice was weaker than usual, and her eyes suddenly looked more tired.

'Are you OK, Not-Granny?' I asked.

She smiled. 'You're such a caring young lady, Charligh. Never change. Yes, I'll be all right, but unfortunately I'm feeling a little under the weather. It's been a busy week for me, what with the musical at the weekend, extra gardening on Sunday and now this, but I am SO glad I came.'

She stopped and took my hand in hers. 'Here's what I really wanted to tell you – your vocals are amazing. I know a chill will run right through the audience when you begin to sing. And I'm really enjoying seeing you up there acting and singing ... but I can feel you're holding something back.'

'I know, I know. I'm wooden,' I said miserably.

Not-Granny shook her head. 'I think that you're still using your head a little too much to remember those lines. You worked hard to learn them, and I'm so proud of you for that. But it's also important for us to see that PIZZAZZ that only YOU can bring to the part of Anne. Sometimes you just need to forget your audience and create your own world.'

She leaned on her stick a little just as we saw Nari wave at us through the window. Not-Granny gave her a nod.

'You'll find your own way, I know you will,' she murmured, before giving me a warm hug. 'Now it's time for you to go back out on that stage . . . and it's time for me to get some rest back at Flora House,' she said with a soft smile.

'Thank you, Not-Granny,' I said. 'I don't know what I would have done without all your wise words and without you being here today . . . !'

Then Not-Granny gave my hand one last squeeze and walked slowly over to meet Nari.

Knowing Not-Granny was in the audience to support me seemed to have given me some confidence, like a real-life mascot or lucky charm. Once she was gone, the second half of the dress rehearsal went terribly.

I'd spent so much time rehearsing the first half – maybe over-rehearsing, if what Summer said had any truth in it – it felt like I hadn't memorized the second half at all, even though I had. I knew I had. I preferred wooden to this.

By the time we reached the finale, 'A Million Annes' was all over the place. I was going left when I was supposed to be going right, clapping low when I was meant to be snapping my fingers high, shuffling when I was meant to be spinning.

It couldn't have gone more wrong, and Summer outshone me in every single way. No matter how hard I tried, it still wasn't coming together quite how I needed it to. I hated to say it, but maybe the Charligh Show wouldn't be going on.

25

An Obstacle Course

After the disastrous dress rehearsal on Friday, I was glad of the distraction of football training over the weekend, even if it did involve an obstacle course. I wasn't overly keen on them because:

1. I found them confusing.
2. There was usually a part where I ended up falling flat on my face.
3. I was ALWAYS last.

The obstacle course was at an outdoor activity centre near Bramrock called Kidz Go Wild. We'd done it before and, yes, I had come last, partly because it involved heaps of dribbling – not my strong point.

At the start of the course, Miss Williams and Rhiannon had set up the cones to be wide apart, but then the closer you came to the end, the narrower the spaces between them got – so you had to make sure your dribbling was really tight.

The second part involved a long, stretchy play tube, but instead of just crawling along it you had to shoot the ball through first, then crawl after it. And it didn't stop there – once you'd collected the ball at the other end of the tube, you had to face someone in goal. Whether you scored or not, you then continued on to the final section of the course where the cones were arranged so that you had to snake down the pitch, then go round in circles, then dribble diagonally . . . and even backwards! Finally, on the very last stretch, you had to hop between two rows of tyres, which, of course, I was especially slow and hopeless at. It was a really tough course!

When Jaz and Talia went round, they dribbled fast and did ball tricks – it was like a great performance you couldn't take your eyes off. Steph went down the tyre run so quickly it was unbelievable, and Allie pulled herself along the tube in a flash after kicking her ball through first time. Layla completed the last stretch flawlessly in a super-quick time of three minutes and forty-seven seconds – which was twice as fast as it had taken me when I'd done the course previously, I noted glumly.

I shrugged. This wasn't as embarrassing as fluffing the play. Everyone knew I was the worst player in the Bramrock Stars. Then I thought of what Not-Granny said: 'Sometimes you just need to forget your audience and create your own world.'

So I did, and this time I pretended I was a superhero stepping up to a challenge with confidence as Talia ran up to me. She high-fived me and the clock began.

'Go on, Charligh!' cheered Miss Williams encouragingly from the middle of the obstacle course, where she was positioned with her whistle and stopwatch.

Normally when I went round the course, I was a bit like a car running out of petrol, slowly chuntering along, but somehow this time I was flying! Before I knew it, I was dribbling down the home stretch. All the twists and turns felt familiar this time, and for once I didn't have to try so hard not to look completely goofy.

'Four minutes and seven seconds, Charligh,' Miss Williams said. 'Brilliant!'

'I can't believe that,' I gasped, collapsing on the bench next to Steph and Jaz as we watched Naomie take her turn.

'I can,' said Jaz. 'You flew through that – you smashed my time anyway!'

'Whatever you did to improve – keep on doing it, Charligh. That was ace!' Rhiannon said.

I'd been focused on the drills for once, instead of performing for everyone watching, and it had really paid off. It's weird – as an actor, I always felt I should be super aware of the audience, even when playing my favourite sport, but the one time I didn't it seemed I'd given my very best performance, and I was super proud of it!

All seven of us Dreamers had completed the obstacle course, and, although it was the same journey, we'd used very different styles and methods to get through it. We'd had to find our own way, and it was amazing to see.

And my success on the course got me thinking. Not-Granny had said we all take different paths, and that I'd have to find my own way with the play. But how?

That evening, after dinner, I decided to visit one of the websites Dr Lincoln had mentioned. I clicked through to the home page of one that had a section called 'Understanding Dyspraxia'.

Dyspraxia is a disorder affecting the fine and gross motor coordination in children and adults. It refers to people who have additional problems planning, organizing and carrying out movements in the right order. It also affects memory, perception and processing.

My finger moved slowly along the lines, and I read the final line out loud. 'Dyspraxia can also affect articulation and speech, perception, thought and memory.'

What kind of actor will I be if I can't do things

in the right order? I thought. *And we already know I'm having trouble remembering my lines . . .*

I bit my lip, suddenly worried.

There was so much information that I decided to divide it up into a list of strengths and weaknesses about being dyspraxic, just like we did with our football game in some training sessions.

Strengths	Weaknesses
• Determined	• Balancing
• Persistent	• Structuring written work
• Hard-working	• Copying information
• Good long-term memory	• Spatial awareness
• Working well independently	• Following multi-step instructions
• Problem-solving	• Organizational skills
• Creativity	• Short-term memory
• Strategic planning	• Non-verbal communication and understanding social etiquette
• Ability to hyper-focus	

I felt good writing it all down. Looking at that list, there was a lot I related to – some of it good, some of it a challenge. Then I summarized what acting was about – reading, movement, line-learning and organization. According to the list, these were all things that might be terribly difficult for me, but not impossible. As well as Daniel Radcliffe, I'd discovered two other actors who had dyspraxia, and Stephanie Guidera, who was a classical singer. I even found two politicians with dyspraxia. They had to make speeches and remember things all the time, didn't they? So there had to be hope for me! Now I had to figure out what the best way for me to learn was. The answer, I knew, was there somewhere – I just had to dig deep.

I took out my phone and lay back on my bed, thinking hard about what might work for me. I hit record on my phone and started setting down my ideas in an audio file. I thought I'd just say everything that came into my head and see if anything made sense afterwards.

Then I played it back and drew up a really good list of new things to try. One of them was writing down my stage directions in a different way. I had to know exactly where I was going and what movement to make. So instead of 'walk to the left', it could be 'walk towards Matthew

Cuthbert'. It would also really help me if the font for the script was bigger and clearer – I'd see if Dodson could print me a new copy. And, instead of cue cards with only a few words on them, maybe there could be a picture on them if I got confused? You know, like a drawing of one of the scenes! *That would really help*, I thought, feeling excited.

Something else occurred to me. All this time, I hadn't been very honest with Dodson. I'd let him think I was a bit lazy instead of telling him the truth. I couldn't have worked any harder than I had done, learning the lines – it was all I'd thought of, and I'd given it my best. But he didn't know that. Now, to get the support I needed, I was going to have to be brave and do something I didn't always like doing – ask for help.

26

A Reasonable Adjustment

The next morning I went straight to Dodson's office and gave him my list of ideas of ways to make it easier for me to learn my lines.

'There's something I need to tell you. The thing is ... I have been trying my hardest to learn my lines and the choreography. At the beginning, I was getting distracted, it's true, but even when I settled down and really gave it my all I still couldn't get anything to stick,' I said to Dodson.

He looked at me quizzically. 'You sound as if you're confessing to something, Charligh. Trying hard is a good thing, isn't it?'

I looked down and shuffled my feet awkwardly. 'Yes ... but being onstage playing the lead has been my biggest dream since, well, forever. I thought it would come easily. And, when it didn't, I didn't want anyone to think I'd cracked under the pressure, or I just wasn't good enough to play Anne. So I suppose it was easier to pretend I wasn't staying up late rehearsing my lines all the time. Sometimes even when I was in the middle of football practice!'

Dodson chuckled. 'I'm sure that went well!'

I smiled. 'Things haven't exactly gone the way I planned, both off and on the pitch. But I still believe that, just like Anne, I can reach the place I need to get to.'

Dodson nodded. 'Well, all these suggestions on your list are great, and I definitely think we can make it work. And let's go through the script together and see if we can make some other changes to help you. You have a real ear for dialogue, and, if you do get stuck, you could also try some improvisation, so long as it's along the same lines as the script. We don't want to trip the other actors up.'

'We can do that?' I said in surprise. I really should have spoken up earlier!

Dodson spread the pages out across the table and stroked his beard thoughtfully.

'There's something else too. When I was in drama school, there was a man who told us about this app called Stage Lines that was actually really helpful for all of us. He happened to be dyslexic and said it made a real difference. Instead of relying solely on reading his lines, he could listen to them when he was on the train, in the car, even in the bath.'

I sighed. 'Thank you, sir, that sounds great. I'm so relieved. I thought you were going to say you'd have to give my part to Summer.'

'That wouldn't work,' Dodson said matter-of-factly. 'I don't think there's anyone in this entire class who could bring to the role what you have. And, similarly, what Summer brings to the role of Diana is unique. With all the challenges you're facing, you've done so well to learn such a huge chunk of your lines. Now you just need to start polishing them to really make sure you deliver them with confidence – and that you're in the right scene at all times!'

It was as if a special box of understanding had been locked up, and now someone had given me the key to open it. Over the next few days, I learned my lines in a way that worked for me. I was memorizing them in a fraction of the time it had taken me before, and now they were really sticking. I didn't have to close my eyes to remember them, or do an emergency scrabble-around in my head.

Mum had helped me find and download the Stage Lines app. And Dodson was right: it was brilliant. Recording everyone's lines really helped me get into what each scene was about line by line, so they were no longer just vague ideas. I could even record where I wanted to add stage directions and colour-code things. I highlighted my bits in green so they stood out.

I'd had to duck out of two football practices, and, sure, Jaz did sound frosty when I texted her (if you can sound frosty in a text), but she'd get over it. I knew this football thing was a huge deal to her ... but there was absolutely nothing wrong with having my own dreams, I thought stubbornly as I lay in bed, reading the script alongside an audio-recorded version in the Stage Lines app.

Jaz had invited us all for a pre-match evening at her house. If you're wondering what that is, it involves:

1. Eating a lot of snacks.
2. Watching clips of games.
3. Pausing and discussing them.

The first thing was definitely enjoyable, but I was less keen on the other two parts of the evening so I'd declined politely with something vague about helping out with the Tinies. It's not as if I was lying, because I *had* decided to entertain them. That's why I was dressed up in a top hat and a glittery blue dress – my special magician's outfit – waving Rory's plastic drumstick as a wand while chanting *abracadabra* and pulling different stuffed toys out of the air (from behind the settee – shh! Don't tell the babies).

Of course, this delicate trick only worked if the twins stayed in front of the settee, and Reuben – the more curious of the two – kept trying to run behind it. Dad was reading on the other sofa and kept laughing at my efforts – he was no help!

Eventually, I got them settled and was beginning my magic act AGAIN when Mum came into the room with her phone in her hand. She sat down on the settee.

'Charligh, can you come over here for a minute?' she said. She looked a bit tearful, and somehow I just knew it was going to be very, very bad news.

'It's Not-Granny, isn't it?' I said. I don't know how I knew, but I just did.

'Yes, it is, sweetie,' Mum said softly. 'I'm so sorry to tell you this, love, but she died peacefully in her sleep last night. I think she'd been unwell for quite a while, and more than she was letting on.' Mum looked at me closely before pulling me in for a hug.

Dad had put down his book and sat a twin on each knee in an effort to keep them quiet while Mum spoke to me. 'I know this isn't the news any of us wanted to hear,' he said, 'but I'm sure you helped to make the last few months of her life really wonderful. You were both very lucky to meet each other.'

'I'm OK,' I said after a pause.

I didn't know what to say or feel, to be honest. But, right at that moment, I didn't want to think about anything that was to do with death or funerals or Not-Granny not being here. It just didn't seem right, though. I wasn't an expert in death or anything, but how could someone look so alive and happy one week, then the next week just be gone?

Mum didn't say anything more. She just sat for a while with her arms round me and kissed the top of my head. Mum had said I was lucky, but I didn't feel I was. I actually didn't feel anything. But I didn't think I'd go back to Flora House ... What was the point? Everyone there was so old, and they were all going to die soon, and it would just make it worse if I got to know them.

That night we ate chicken-and-mushroom pie in silence. It was as if even Rory and Reuben knew something had changed. They were quieter than they'd been for a long while, but still, everything felt so loud. I could hear Dad going chomp-chomp-chomp. I could hear the twins mush-mush-biting into pastry and vegetables, and Mum's quiet nattering about all the coursework she had to mark by Monday.

'Could you please just ... shh!' I burst out, exasperated by everyone.

'Charligh,' Mum said, 'I know you're upset – it's really tough losing Betty – but lashing out at us isn't like you ...'

I frowned. 'It doesn't matter. Not-Granny was old anyway. The problem is that the twins don't know how to eat quietly.'

Mum looked like she was about to say something, but Dad interrupted. 'I think what Charligh is trying to say is that Betty had a long, happy and successful life, and was lucky enough to live to a good age.'

I nodded – that *was* what I'd been trying to say, kind of – then sipped at my glass of milk because something suspiciously like a lump was forming in my throat. *A piece of chicken must have gone down the wrong way*, I thought, stubbornly spearing another chunk with my fork.

Mum still looked worried. 'Do you still definitely want to go to football tomorrow? I know it's an important game and all, but I'm sure the others would understand if you're not feeling OK.'

'I'm fine, honestly I am. And sorry for snapping at you all – especially the babies.' I blew Reuben and Rory kisses.

It didn't matter what I did or didn't feel. I knew I was going to turn up on the pitch tomorrow for our very important game. I was a Dreamer, and we never give up.

27

A Mighty Battle

Today was super important for everyone, but especially Jaz and Allie since it was their chance to really impress the scouts. There was a good crowd too – nearly everyone's parents had come to see us play against our old rivals, the Silverstone Shiners, and this time we were on home ground.

Rory and Reuben were in their raincoats and wellies, sitting in the double buggy with the plastic cover pulled over them, and Mum and Dad were standing under their massive golf umbrella, shielding themselves from the on-and-off drizzle.

I stood in our huddle, waiting for Rhiannon to finish talking. 'Mandy and Raine, the two women standing over there at the corner with the clipboards, are the Soccer School scouts. I know not all of you have an interest in going to Soccer School, let alone progressing to an academy, but the better we all play, the better it looks for Allie and Jaz. And, if we win this game, we're still in with a chance of coming first in the league.'

'There's no *if* about it,' said Allie. 'We've got to win this game!'

Jaz nodded. 'There's no reason why we can't beat them again.'

I stretched my arms upwards, partly to distract myself because Allie and Jaz were making me feel even more nervous.

This morning I'd felt stiff and heavy. *It's probably just the weather*, I thought, looking at the wet-charcoal sky. The Dreamers had heard about Not-Granny and asked if I was OK when we were getting changed. I'd said yes. I didn't really know what else to say, and I wasn't sure how I was supposed to feel. I'd expected some tears yesterday – I'd even placed a big box of tissues next to my bed – but they never seemed to come. I suppose I was stronger than I thought.

I shrugged away the guilt I felt at not shedding a tear for Not-Granny.

'Don't forget we're playing the new formation for the first half,' said Miss Williams.

I groaned, pulling my arms down from the stretch. 'Midfield again!'

'You'll be fine,' said Steph encouragingly.

'OK ... the rain has stopped, and the game's starting!' said Talia.

'It's a sign!' said Layla, smiling, her face wet with rain.

'Let's go, Dreamers!' said Naomie, following Jaz, who had already run out on to the pitch, raring to go. I sighed inwardly, wishing I had even half her enthusiasm.

I stumbled down the wing, trying desperately to gain ground on the super-fast winger I was marking. She slammed the ball in, making it 3–2 to the Shiners. Jaz had quickly scored two goals in the first ten minutes, but the Shiners weren't giving up without a fight, and had summoned skills and a strength we hadn't seen from them before to get three balls into our goal. We'd never conceded that many during the first half of any other match this season. If this continued, the Dreamers would be obliterated, annihilated and erased from the earth, or at least the top spot of the league, and the scouts wouldn't give Jaz or Allie a second glance.

But what was worse was that inside I felt everything was unravelling, like a thread uncoiling from a spool, but I couldn't see how to stop it. I was so glad to hear the whistle go at half-time. We trooped over towards Rhiannon and Miss Williams, and stood underneath one of the shelters as the rain got heavier.

'Is everything OK, Charligh?' Steph said gently.

My cheeks burned. 'What do you mean?'

'All the forwards kept whizzing past you,' said Talia.

'Well, they kept whizzing past Allie too or doesn't that count?' I retorted.

'Don't blame me –' started Allie.

'Hang on. Let's all just focus on beating the Shiners and keep our attacks directed at them,' Naomie said levelly.

'Yes, come on – we can still do this,' said Layla. 'I know we're all trying our best, so there's no point blaming each other. And whatever happens, we're still winners, remember?'

'Exactly,' said Rhiannon, looking thoughtful (though Jaz appeared unconvinced). 'OK, let's do a bit of a swap – Charligh, we'll have you back on defence and Layla in midfield.'

I should have been pleased really, since going back to my old position is what I wanted. But suddenly I could hear a voice in my head . . . and it was calling me a LOSER! Rhiannon obviously knew I was hopeless, so she was moving me to a different position, hoping that things would get better, but they wouldn't.

I chewed my lip, agitated. What would happen when Rhiannon realized this was the best she would get from me?

As we started the second half, the on-and-off rain exploded into a torrential downpour. We were no strangers to playing in the rain so it wasn't going to be a problem for us. But it soon became very clear that the Shiners were used to it too, as it didn't slow down their efforts at all.

Shot after shot came at our goal, so we were forced into playing a defensive game.

Finally, Steph managed to break through their defence and passed the ball at the last minute to Talia, who dribbled it round the girl marking her and blasted it in. Yes! We were back in with a fighting chance. The score was now 3–3, and we had everything to play for. If we could show those scouts that we could turn a defeat into a win, that would be enough to make up for our performance in the first half. And we would go out with our heads held high, having defended our title of reigning champions against our rivals, the Shiners!

And then, with one minute to go, Jill Hutchinson intercepted a throw-in from me that was meant to land at Layla's feet, but hadn't quite reached her. Before I could even blink twice, Jill had darted round me and taken a shot at goal. It was a long shot, but her path was clear, and we all held our breath as the ball made its journey. I saw Allie dive for it, but it bounced off the top of the goalpost and landed in the back of the net.

Jaz looked dejected and Allie furious. It was the seventh and final goal of the match: 4–3. We'd needed to win this, or at the very least scrape a draw, but instead we'd lost. So much for helping Allie and Jaz shine in front of the scouts.

As the final whistle went, I felt myself sinking down on to the grass. Something hot and painful inside me floated to the surface and – before I knew what was happening – bubbled over. My shoulders heaved as my hands dug into the wet mud. I was a loser. I'd lost the game for everyone – just like I'd ruined the play. It was as if a storm had erupted inside me, and as lightning-hot tears spilled out I realized I wasn't only crying about the match.

'I want her back,' I bawled. I could see the Shiners looking curiously at me, but for once I didn't want to be seen. I didn't want to be the centre of attention. What I wanted was to melt away under the avalanche of feelings that had come rolling down on me. I was at my lowest, and I didn't know how to get up.

But then all of a sudden I felt arms round me, holding me tight. It was Steph, pulling me to my feet, then Jaz holding me up on the other side.

I peeked over her shoulder and could see Layla and Allie had wrapped their arms round me too – round all of us – and they stood, linked together, to keep me from falling. Talia was on the outside. She wasn't much for hugging, but she had grabbed my hand and was squeezing it tight.

I'd told them at the start of our game that I was OK, and I didn't miss Not-Granny. But now I knew they hadn't believed me. And I was glad.

My team didn't ask any questions as they stood with me, surrounding me and holding me up like a circle of strength.

Back home and in the bath, I leaned against the cushioned bath pillow and inhaled the eucalyptus bubble bath that had steamed up the whole bathroom. The twins had seen I was upset, and Reuben had insisted Mum let me play with their rubber bath turtles. I would normally have said no, but this time I was grateful. I remembered some facts Steph had told me about real turtles when we'd been to the London Aquarium in Year 4. They are Testudines, a kind of reptile, so they're in the same family as tortoises and terrapins too. And some of them are old, like really old. They often live to a be a hundred.

Not-Granny would have been a hundred in eleven years.

I started sobbing again, glad I was in the bathroom away from everyone, though I knew Mum was camped outside the door. Usually, I'd roll my eyes, but this time I gave a tiny smile – she'd been so worried about me since my meltdown earlier at football.

After everyone had finally let go of me, Mum and Dad had dashed over, swept me up in a blanket and bundled me into the back of the car. Reuben and Rory were strangely quiet, as if they knew something was wrong. That had made me feel bad, so I'd cried some more.

I suppose you can't act your way out of everything. Once I realized that, I felt crushed, but also somehow relieved. Like the mask I'd been wearing had finally been removed, and I could breathe properly again.

When I came out of the bathroom, my skin red-raw, bundled up in my huge towelling robe with my hair wrapped in a towel too, my little brother came rushing out of his room darting round a frazzled-looking Mum.

'Char-ree!' Reuben said happily.

I couldn't believe it! He'd just said his first word! And it was me – it was *my* name.

Mum gasped and yelled out for Dad to come and see, while I started crying all over again as I lifted my little brother into my arms and cuddled him gently. I knew he could hear the words in that silent squeeze.

Love you.

28

A Message From Not-Granny

If yesterday the weather was crying with me, today it was smiling down at me.

It was hard to believe there'd been a full-blown thunderstorm yesterday. Today the spring sunshine warmed my face as I stepped out of the shade and on to the sun-splashed patio. A few months ago, the rock garden at Flora House had been a pile of crumbly soil and weeds. Now it boasted a circus of purple irises, yellow daffodils and flame-orange tulips, and everything was sprinkled with cherry-blossom petals, covering it in a kind of coral glitter.

I put my sunglasses on and stared up at the sky, pausing for a moment. It was the colour of pink, fleshy fruit with streaks of orange, apricot and red at the edges, and bold white lines ran through it, crisscrossing each other like endless paths. Then I looked back down at the little package next to me on the bench where Not-Granny and I had usually sat.

This morning Mum told me that Nari had called and said Not-Granny had a present for me. She'd been planning to give it to me as an early birthday present the night of the final performance of *Anne and Friends*. The package was covered in rose-gold wrapping, and it had a translucent pink ribbon round it tied in a tiny bow. Nari had offered to drop it off, but I'd decided to come and open it here, in the place where Not-Granny and I had met most often.

My eyes wandered to the end of the bench, which was now empty. No Not-Granny today or ever again. Yet her words came to me loud and clear: *Enjoy every season*.

I pulled the ribbon loose and unwrapped it slowly, opening the box up to find a long, thin envelope, a small jewellery box and a thick journal with tiny sunflowers on it. Then, hidden under the journal, I saw a slim rectangular gift box and inside that was a chunky, crocodile-green pen. I pulled it out from the box and ran my thumb along the smooth metal until I reached the top of the pen, where there was a gem-encrusted butterfly design. I looked at each item for a little while before tearing the envelope open to find a card written in Not-Granny's spindly but grand handwriting.

To the fabtastic Charligh with a 'gh',

It's one of my biggest boasts to say that I got to spend a lot of the last three months of my eighty-ninth year with you. At first, I thought you reminded me of a younger me, but then I realized you weren't that. You were something far better — your own special, unique you — and it was magnificent. Thank you for being you.

Alas, I don't have riches or gold to give you like a generous benefactor in the classic movies that we so love to watch, but I want you to have this special bracelet. It's made of pearl, real, finest pearl (at least that's what my Great-Aunty Jocelyn said), but, even if it's not, please know that my sentiments are. Every time you wear it, I want you to remember to be as authentic as possible. Under the layers of gloss and shine, there's still an unpolished gem and, indeed, under all our glamour, that is what we all are.

   Now there's not much more to say except break a leg . . . and shine on, Charligh!

Yours truly,

Not-Granny (aka Betty Langton)

A showreel of our best moments together ran through my head, and I could just see it, every scene a happy moment in the short time we'd known each other. Sitting on the bench, watching the winter garden blossom, our first duet, sipping Golden Tea, dreaming about my future in acting, our shared love of felines.

Now I finally understood what Dad meant about the power of the written word. There was no audio, no music, no lights, no audience, and yet a zillion sparks of inspiration had been lit inside me. Not-Granny had left me the BEST gift.

I opened the journal and discovered a little slip of paper inside.

For writing about yourself where Nancy-from-across-the-road can't see you.

And now a canyon of laughter split through the desert inside me, and in it a stream of burbling happiness rose up and overflowed. Instead of sadness, I now felt very grateful that I had got the chance to meet someone as special, kind and funny as Not-Granny.

'We were worried about you,' Jaz said. Steph and Naomie were sitting either side of her on my bed.

'And we come bearing gifts,' added Steph solemnly. 'I picked these for you from my garden.' She handed me a bunch of pale lemon primroses wrapped in paper. They were beautiful.

Naomie opened a large zipped bag and passed over the presents to me one by one. There was a plastic tub full of vanilla cupcakes Jaz had baked, and a handmade card from Effie with a picture of a girl with long red hair (that was supposed to be me) standing next to a big yellow sun.

'The whole team is worried. Talia and Allie feel especially guilty, like maybe they'd piled too much pressure on you and tipped you over the edge. And here – Layla wrote you one of those haiku poems to help cheer you up, and Allie has illustrated it,' Jaz said, handing over a small rectangle of paper.

Naomie pulled the last item out of the bag. 'Some spiced tea. Talia thinks you'll love it. It's her and her gran's favourite. And we have some very good news about yesterday, by the way.' She shared a quick grin with Jaz. 'Jaz and Allie were both accepted on to Summer Soccer School!'

I squealed as I pulled Jaz in for a big hug. 'Congratulations, that's amazing! You're one step closer to playing at Wembley. I'll miss you – you'd better video-call me every day. And let me know if you spot anyone famous in London!'

Jaz grinned. 'I'm so excited! And, yeah, it sucks that we won't be walking away with the winner's trophy this season, but if we get at least two draws we've got a very good chance of the runner-up shield.'

'We've been thinking,' said Steph. 'We usually play seven-a-side, but there's only seven of us in the team. And remember what happened to us when I came off with an injury in the final? We had to carry on with just six players.'

Naomie nodded. 'We're vulnerable, and it also piles too much pressure on the team if one of us can't play for any reason.'

I looked at them, holding my breath. Was this the end of the Dreamers? Had I destroyed the world's best girls' seven-a-side football team? I bit my lip in suspense and then exhaled as Jaz broke the news.

'We're going to recruit at least one more Dreamer, and not just anyone. We'll make sure they love football, and they love our team! We don't want any greedy Garys hogging the ball . . .'

'. . . Or selfish Susies who eat all the team cake,' said Naomie, sounding appalled at the very thought of it.

'We'll make sure they're happy with us, and we're happy with them,' said Steph.

'What do you think?' said Naomie.

I smiled. 'I think that's a great idea, but I just have one suggestion ... you'd better not bring on anyone as dramatic as me. I'm not sure even I could survive that!'

It wasn't very much notice – the play was in less than forty-eight hours – but I was sure she'd be happy to finally get her chance in the spotlight. With everything else that was going on, I'd decided that I'd better bow out of the role of Anne. It just didn't feel right with Not-Granny not being here and me bursting into tears all the time. When we got lost in the New Forest, the best thing I'd done was to hand over the map to Steph and let her take the lead.

I'd wanted to play this role for ages, and I'd been so determined, but sometimes the smart thing to do is to step aside and give it to someone who'd do it better. I could see her in the part now, and maybe someone else could be Diana as she had fewer lines. So, as much as I didn't want to, that's why I was standing here, waiting for Summer to come to the door after her mum had called her down. Preparing for the insurmountable challenge of asking her to do me and everyone involved in the play a favour.

I could almost see Summer's disdain mingled with surprise flicker across her face as she came to the door.

'What are you doing here, Charligh Gorley or Green, or whatever it is you're calling yourself nowadays?' she said.

I knew I had about five seconds before she shut the door in my face so I just launched into it.

'I want you to be Anne. You know all the lines, and you can do the choreography properly for "A Million Annes".'

'No,' said Summer.

'No?' I parroted in disbelief.

She's been breathing down my neck and trying to sabotage my chances, and now she says no. Huh?

'Yes, no.' She rolled her eyes at me. 'Also, you look really tired.'

Thanks, Summer, I thought. I was tempted to think of a witty comeback, but I decided the truth would do this time.

'Not-Granny, I mean Betty Langton . . . passed away.' I bit my lip, not able to bring myself to say 'dead' out loud.

Summer could, though. 'She's dead?!' she gasped, sounded genuinely distressed.

I was surprised. I'd forgotten Summer had feelings.

'Stop letting all the flies in,' called Mrs Singh from behind Summer. Summer hesitated for a second, then – to my surprise – invited me in.

This was the first time I'd ever been in Summer's bedroom. I expected it to be the exact opposite of the messiness of my room . . . and it was. Her desk was totally clear except for two neat piles of paper, one of which she told me was dance notation, kind of like sheet music except, instead of musical notes, there was a bunch of symbols for different dance moves. The other pile was the *Anne and Friends* script.

Her bedroom walls were white and bare, except for one blown-up canvas-print photo of Summer and her much older sister who was away at university. Her beige bedspread was perfectly arranged – I felt bad sitting on it.

Mrs Singh brought us some digestives and orange juice, and we talked about our favourite scenes in the play, the trickiest parts, who our favourite characters were (except for our own roles, of course) and also what we thought of Dodson. Summer said she loved him – he was her favourite teacher. I said he'd grown on me.

'Well, we've come a long way since the nativity,' she said in that silent-assassin way of hers.

She was about as subtle as a sledgehammer, and I knew EXACTLY what she was getting at. You see, it wasn't that I cared, not that I'd thought about it often, not that I'd wondered why Summer just ditched me, but still, if she was going to throw in little digs like that, I might as well have it out with her and take a little detour from my mission.

'Why did you stop talking to me?' I asked abruptly.

Summer looked at me curiously and put the last bit of her biscuit down. 'Because I'm eating,' she said in that slow, irritating way again.

'I hate it when you talk to me like that,' I said, annoyed. 'As if I'm stupid. I didn't mean just now – I meant back in Reception class at Cross Grove Infants. After the nativity play? I'd thought we were friends.'

'What?' Summer sprayed out a shower of biscuit crumbs, and her mouth hung open. 'Sorry. I'm just shocked.'

'Me too,' I said, pulling a face. 'That was extremely unpleasant.'

She took a gulp of her juice and wiped her mouth. 'No, not about that – I mean the fact that you're asking me about stuff from Reception class. How do you even remember that far back?'

'Are you trying to say you don't?' I said in disbelief.

There was a short pause. 'OK, what happened as far as I remember was you sabotaged my special moment and then acted as if I didn't exist.'

I gasped. 'I did what?!'

'Sa-bo-taged,' she said, drawing each syllable out. 'I was Mary, and all the attention was supposed to be on me. But you had everyone running around after you, and you were only the donkey. I'm not saying you wet yourself on purpose –' she looked at me rather suspiciously – 'but it did work out rather well for you, centre-of-attention-wise. I wanted to put it all behind me, but then the next day you walked past me as if I didn't exist.'

'That's because you were acting as if *I* didn't exist! And the embarrassment had reached EPIC proportions then,' I said, lowering my voice.

Summer looked thoughtful. 'We must have both ignored each other, I suppose?'

'One great big misunderstanding,' I said, frowning. 'Have you ever seen *Pride and Prejudice*?'

'Yes, I love it! It's one of my favourite films. I kept yelling: "Why don't you just talk to each other?"'

'I've always said that kind of thing doesn't happen in real life, but maybe it does,' I said, giggling. 'Imagine if we had been besties all this time?'

We looked at each other in Summer's mirrored wardrobe and gave an identical grimace at exactly the same time. *Maybe not.*

I put my glass down and turned to Summer.

'So, about playing Anne.' I looked at her hopefully. 'You may have noticed – no, you definitely have noticed – that I've had a horrible time learning my lines. I've done my best, but, let's face it, that's not good enough for a stand-out, stop-the-press kind of show. And that is what we're going for ... aren't we? I mean, the cast didn't work that hard only for the lead to throw it all away with a mediocre performance, did they?'

She nodded slowly and looked as if she was thinking it over.

'I'll play Anne if you really want me to ... but I don't think you do. You care enough about this to ask me to do it because you don't want to mess it up. You've come to every rehearsal, and they haven't all gone perfectly, but you tried. I think you want this more than me, to be honest. Sure, I'd have liked to have been cast as Anne, but I've kind of got used to playing Diana, and I really like her.' She paused. 'And not just because she's the pretty one, but she's just more my kind of person. Anne *is* kind of annoying.'

'She is not!' I said hotly.

Summer gave a pleased smile. 'See? You and Anne are two of a kind. You wouldn't have been my first choice for the part, but now I think you're perfect for the role.' She held up a hand as if we were in a boardroom meeting. 'I vote for Charligh to play Anne Shirley.'

As infuriating as she was being, that did make me smile a bit. I thought about what she'd said. Then I dug deep ... and I pulled it out: a glimmer of hope; a nugget of confidence. Summer was right. I didn't want to sit on the sidelines. Anne was my role, and I was ready to tackle it. I'd just have to find a way through to the end of this journey. My way.

I slowly held up my hand. 'I guess it's unanimous then. I vote for me to play Anne Shirley too. Thank you, Summer,' I added.

We chatted some more. It was weird having our first proper conversation since we were four years old, and I found out a lot. Apparently, Summer prefers dancing to acting and singing. That's why she'd choreographed the dance in the play, not to sabotage me at all as it turns out. Oh, and it was her mum's idea for her to be involved in the play.

'I guess she wants me to be a bit more sociable like her,' Summer said, 'but now she's realized that just isn't me. And we're both OK with that.' She paused. 'You may not be my cup of tea, but you're a bit of a people magnet. I think almost everyone in our class talks to you.'

I nearly laughed out loud because I'd got Summer so wrong in many ways. Not only was I the villain in her version of the nativity story, but there were even things about me she kind of admired.

Silence fell between us, and I could hear her pet hamster whirring round in its wheel. I'd had an idea, and I still needed Summer's help. And the Bramrock Stars.

'Are you free for one more rehearsal tomorrow? A very long one,' I said thoughtfully.

'Sure. I don't have any plans, but I'm not sure about the rest of the cast.'

'That's OK. We don't need them as long as it's you, me and the Dreamers – we'll give them a copy of the script, and they can play the other roles so we can rehearse properly.'

'Spending time with you and all the Dreamers isn't at the top of my bucket list, BUT if you think it'll work, count me in!' said Summer. She stood up and nodded. 'See you tomorrow then.'

I guessed this was my cue to leave.

'See you, Summer,' I said as I closed the bedroom door behind me.

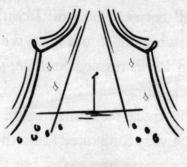

29

The Final Performance

'Welcome to the *Charligh Green Show*. I'm here to discuss all things vintage, beauty tips and the latest gossip straight from Charligh's World.' For the first time ever, I was doing a vlog while still in my pyjamas. Some might call it laziness, but I knew better – it was authentic. Even stars don't look glammed up all day every day!

'Today's the day,' I continued. 'Tonight I'll be making my debut performance in the musical production of *Anne and Friends*, co-written by Dodson and Miss Williams! After a whole day practising yesterday, I'm as ready as I'll ever be. I'm still reeling from the fact we had Summer and the Dreamers working together on something, and not a single soul imploded or exploded. Hmm.'

I tilted my head to one side. 'Maybe we've come one major step closer to world peace – or at least peace in Bramrock. But the real test will be tonight. The odds are fifty-fifty as to whether I sink or swim, but I'm definitely going to dive in and be the very best Anne Shirley I can – and no one can do better than that!'

I clicked the off button on the remote control and gave myself the thumbs up in my mirror. 'It's time to shine on, Charligh Green!'

And now it really was time.

From where I was peeping out from behind the curtain, I could see Mum and Dad right in the middle of the front row. Nari, Antonio and Sylvia had seats in the row behind, and Jaz was sitting at the front in the upper gallery with her family. Somehow she managed to spot me and waved with both hands. I resisted the urge to wave back now that the whole theatre was still and quiet.

To my surprise, Dodson stepped on to the stage and gave a short speech to the audience. He spoke about how this had been the best school production he'd ever been involved in, and how much he had learned as a scriptwriter and director, and especially how much the cast had taught him. He described us as hard-working, diligent and very talented.

The audience applauded. I couldn't believe it! I never thought Dodson would speak so warmly about any of us like that.

I clenched and unclenched my fists and breathed in and out, trying to remember how to root myself here in this moment and not go flying off somewhere else in my thoughts. It was time to get ready. The cast gathered together behind the curtains with just minutes to go until the play started.

Then, finally, it was 7 p.m.

'The beginning,' read Talia as the lights slowly dimmed, and the curtains opened.

I knew this was my moment. I walked out towards the centre of the stage ... and, with perfect timing, broke into the intro song. An electrified silence fell over the audience, and I flew through the rest of it. Finally, I held the last note and hit the falsetto just right.

Take that, stage fright, I thought triumphantly.

But then disaster nearly struck! For a split second, an image of the terrible dress rehearsals popped into my mind ... and I was stuck in freeze-frame. Everyone around me faded to sepia and then black. Panic hit me – but I shut my eyes, and I visualized myself at the rehearsal yesterday doing what I needed to do tonight. I blinked and slowly everything came back into focus, like an old-style photo being developed.

Then I smiled and relaxed my shoulders. Bubbles of words floated inside my head ... and my first line came to me.

'Well, isn't this a charming train station!' I said.

Theo ambled on to the stage with a Matthew Cuthbert shy smile on his face and introduced himself to me.

We got into our fake horse and carriage and began our conversation. We paused for just enough time to let the audience titter quietly and sometimes loudly. In the whole scene, I only forgot one line, but then I saw Jaz waving frantically at me with her picture card to remind me, and it came back!

I sang my final solo, 'Who is Anne Shirley?' in a stripped-back form, not overpowering everyone else or the music, but singing in harmony, about new starts, magical lakes and poetic expression.

The next scenes flew by: meeting Marilla Cuthbert, being miserable at the idea of being sent away, and walking to school for the first time with Gilbert Blythe. Then Summer entered the classroom, and she was absolutely brilliant. She really brought her own self to Diana and played her with Diana's own sweet personality, but with just a little more spark.

And then – I could hardly believe it – it was time for the final number!

We all lined up to do Summer's choreographed dance for 'A Million Annes' … and it was so much fun! Everyone behind me was moving in perfect synchronicity and hitting every step flawlessly, and I had the time of my life, twirling and swaying and snapping my fingers to the rhythm. As I spun round and danced onstage, I realized that actually it's OK to find your own rhythm. We won't always be dancing in unison with others, and maybe we'll look out of step, but that's OK, since sometimes we're marching to a different beat.

I twirled onstage with the spotlight following me right up until the end of the very last note of the song, at which point the audience burst into the biggest cheer ever! The clapping of their hands and the thunder of their stamping feet rang out throughout the theatre as we took our final bow.

It was amazing!!

And I had a surprise up my sleeve.

Anne and Friends might be over, but the performance wasn't over for me and Summer – there was still one more song to go.

Once the audience had quietened down a bit, I stepped back into the spotlight. My voice cracked but I kept going.

'Betty Langton was my Not-Granny. She was supposed to be here tonight, and I'm sure she would have loved joining us up onstage. Unfortunately, she passed away last week. Since she's not here, and you may not have been lucky enough to meet her, I wanted to say a few words about her.

'She loved cats, almost as much as I do, and we even went to see *Cats* the musical together. She was a very talented actor and singer, and many of her former students from the drama schools where she taught have called her an iconic legend.

'She always told me to be myself – I know that may sound obvious, but if you think about it you'll see that many of us think we're better off if we pretend to be something we're not. And, when you're an actor, you can get lost in a performance, pretending to be someone else, but the best thing you can be, even when you're playing other roles, is authentic.

'I don't have any other thoughts I'd like to share so I'd better get on with the singing bit,' I said. 'This song is in honour of Betty Langton, and I'll be performing it as a duet with my co-star, Summer Singh!'

Then Allie came and sat down onstage with her djembe drum and began the beat. It seemed to go on forever until the speaker music started to play, blending perfectly with the drumbeat. Then the supporting actors – as well as the Dreamers – came from backstage to form the chorus, and Summer stood next to me. I felt scared, but more alive than ever and, as we began, I could feel those emotions pulsing through me.

And then, at the familiar words of 'Circle of Life': *'Ingonyama nengw' enamabala'*, I found myself closing my eyes, waiting to harmonize and blend with Summer as I swayed to the music and began to sing about life, death, beginnings and endings, hope and despair, high suns and sapphire skies.

Finally, I got to the last line. I sang alone, and I held the last word – 'life' – longer and stronger than I ever had before because I think that's what life deserved – especially Not-Granny's.

As I opened my eyes I could see everyone who could had stood up to clap, and those who couldn't rattled their walking sticks, if they had one, or tapped the side of their seats, and a brilliant cacophony of noise filled the room – and it was just as well because I was crying again. I had sung my entire heart out, but it had been worth it.

I felt both sadness and happiness mingled together. I didn't know they could coexist like that, simultaneously swirling and whirling inside and pouring out of me. I figured this river of grief wouldn't just evaporate. It would always be there, but, like water, it would change form: sometimes to frost, sometimes like solid ice, and at other times like steam, barely perceptible. But it being there didn't mean it would overpower the still-strong sea of happiness that also surged within me.

30

A Special Talk

'That was amazing, cast! You should all give yourselves a huge pat on the back! Thank you so much for all your hard work. The way everyone came together and made each part their own was just perfect.' Dodson paused, looking over at me and Summer. 'Though I didn't realize the two of you would be improvising some of the scenes.'

I opened my mouth to defend Summer, as it had all been my idea. I thought it was a good way of bringing more 'me' to the role. Plus, it was my best chance at remembering all the lines in such a short space of time.

But Dodson held up a hand to stop me. 'Nor did I expect Charligh to be freestyling during the last dance routine.'

He pinched the bridge of his nose and closed his eyes briefly. Uh-oh. Was he cross? Had I ruined everything after all?

'Thank you. It really turned a great school play into an unforgettable one. And, when I move on to a new school next term, I won't forget any of you.' He gestured round at all of us, smiling the biggest smile I'd ever seen on his face!

I breathed a sigh of relief and exchanged a quiet smile with my co-star, Summer.

'What was it you were going to say, Charligh?' Dodson turned to me.

I grinned. 'Nothing. Just thank you for being the best director ever.'

He smiled. 'My next school will have a tough act to follow!'

'Do you feel ready?' asked Mum the next morning.

I nodded as I cut the last half-slice of my French

toast into three tiny triangles before chopping a banana on to the plate.

'I've got my flashcards, my presentation is uploaded to my laptop, and I've been through it twice already.'

'I'm very impressed by how organized you've been,' Dad said. 'You worked so hard on this, starting with some squiggles on a page, and here we are now!'

'Wish your sister good luck,' said Mum to Reuben, whose legs were swinging from the chair next to her.

He gave me a sticky smile, his cheeks glistening with the jam from his toast. 'Gooluk, Charligh,' he cooed. He was saying my name perfectly now, and Mum and Dad's, and a whole lot of other words too. Reuben was going to end up being as big a chatterbox as me, and I loved it.

'Char-ree,' Rory echoed.

I blew Reuben and Rory kisses as I got up from the table to grab my bag and jacket before I headed off to school.

'Thanks, Tinies. I'll need it.'

*

'We have had so many wonderful solo talks this term,' Miss Williams said. 'It takes real guts to put yourself out there and talk about something you're passionate about. Thank you, Steph, for yesterday's talk on sea pollution and your tips on what we can do to speak out against climate change. Today Charligh is doing a special presentation about what she's learned on her acting journey.'

My presentation was all set up on the laptop and connected to the whiteboard. I reached down into my schoolbag and took out the masquerade mask I'd made at Meaden Lodge.

I walked slowly but confidently to the front of the class. Usually, I got nervous about not acting well enough, but today it was because I wasn't going to act at all, and everyone was going to see me. The *real* me.

I put the laptop down on Miss Williams's desk, then picked up the mask and arranged my prompt cards in front of me. It felt like a story was about to unfold, and I suppose that's what it was. The story of me. Not all of my stories, but one of them.

There was gentle murmuring and fidgeting, and everyone looked fairly uninterested – everyone except for Jaz, Naomie, Steph and Talia, who were all giving me a thumbs up. I was sure, amid the sniggering from Zach and his friends, that I heard one of them say, 'Why's she dressed as Batman?' but I decided to ignore them.

Miss Williams cleared her throat and gave the class a pointed look, waiting for the murmuring and giggles to die down.

Then she smiled encouragingly at me. 'Go ahead, Charligh.'

I switched my presentation to the title page, and picked up my first prompt card, the sweaty pads of my fingers sticking slightly to the paper. Then I took a deep breath . . . and began.

'Today I'm here to talk about what I learned on my road to being an actor. When I first chose acting as my topic, I expected to be talking about Daphne Dabello. She's my favourite actress, and she has her own set of golden rules, that used to be mine too.'

I put down the card and stretched my hands out flat on the desk and stared at my nails. 'But I found out along the way that those rules weren't working for me, not if I wanted to become the kind of actor that I realized I did want to be.

Because, you see, once you take to the stage and play a part, it's not just "acting" or "singing" – you're telling a story that has the power to make people laugh or cry and think and maybe change their ideas. It might make others see things from a different perspective, and that's very important for developing empathy.' I clicked through to the definition of empathy: *The ability to understand and share the feelings of another.*

'When I first began rehearsals, I thought it would be plain sailing, but I soon found out that learning lines was really hard for me. Suddenly I was dreading nearly every rehearsal and worrying if I was going to be able to do the one thing I've always loved, which is being onstage. That made me feel a bit useless and silly . . . until I found out that I had something called dyspraxia.'

I peeked out from over the card, searching everyone's faces. They still looked interested. *Phew!*

'You might be wondering what dyspraxia is? Well, it's basically just a different way of thinking and doing things. The more official definition is that it's a condition that affects a person's fine and gross motor coordination, memory and movement. This can make things like writing, learning to swim or riding a bike more difficult, and it can also affect speech, perception and thought, among other things.'

I clicked the screen to show everyone the neurodivergence umbrella, which displayed the overlap and differences between other kinds of neurodivergence, including dyslexia, dysgraphia and dyscalculia.

'Most of you in this room are probably neurotypical, because neurotypical people make up the majority of the population. It doesn't mean you're any more or less special or smart; it just means your way of thinking is more common. So, the world is kind of set up for neurotypicals, which is why learning more about dyspraxia helped me understand why I sometimes struggle to do things that seem easy to others.

'It was like in a movie when a light bulb comes on in the main character's head. It explained why I lose my place when I read things, why my writing looks like a spidery scrawl with tons of mistakes, and why I fall over and bump into things more times than my toddler brothers who've only just learned to walk.'

A ripple of laughter went through the classroom as I made eye contact with everyone for the first time. I stood up from the seat and loosened up immediately. 'And then there's the other side of dyspraxia, which for me is a lot about this mask I wear.'

I untied my mask carefully and laid it on the desk.

'Unlike the one I just took off, you can't see it, but it makes me mimic people without even realizing, or camouflage my feelings so people don't see how frustrated, or sad, or even angry I am over something. And sometimes I don't really understand what I'm feeling because of the way my brain processes things. I wear it so much that I sometimes forget I even have it on, but it's so much more comfortable than not wearing a mask. I don't even know why I started wearing it. I suppose it's because I was terrified of being the awkward caterpillar when I really wanted to be a butterfly, but at the same time I was worried about what people would think about the real me. So I went out of my way to put on the best performance you've ever seen, all the time. And that was EXHAUSTING,' I said, with a loud sigh.

I flicked to the second-to-last slide. It was a team picture Rhiannon had taken of us. I smiled. I hadn't shown this bit to the Dreamers when I'd practised with them.

'This is my team, the Bramrock Stars. I like playing football – it's a lot of fun, and it helps me keep fit, and that's important if you want to sing and dance in the West End one day. But my favourite thing about it is definitely my teammates. There's Jaz, our team captain – she's so brave. When they told her girls couldn't play football, her response was to start a team up herself! She also happens to be my best bestie.

'Then there's Steph – she looks after everyone on and off the pitch, which makes her a great team secretary. She's also helped us to be more environmentally conscious, and her love of doing things for charity helps me to care more about others too.

'Naomie's so clever and knows just about everything to do with maths and the stars and space – and one day I'll be able to tell people one of my best friends is a rocket scientist, which is SUPER cool.

'Is there a *Mastermind* just for chess? If so, I nominate my friend Talia to go on it. She knows all the rules, as well as those for literally every game and sport invented – even the ones she doesn't play. I used to think she loved rules for the sake of it, but it's actually because she values fairness – and I don't know about you, but I think that's amazing.

'Then there's Layla. She's probably going to publish a book of poetry one day because she's written a zillion poems already, but, unlike me, she's very humble and reluctant to show off her talent. I think, when she does, it will change the world – because that's what words do.

'And last but not least is Allie.' I paused for breath. 'Now, I wouldn't say we share the same taste in anything other than football, but I love how she really doesn't hold back. Unlike with other people, I never have to figure out what Allie's thinking because she never stops herself from saying what she thinks, or worries about being too polite.

'I know this is a talk about me and my dyspraxia, but this team of my very favourite friends has helped me celebrate my differences and accept that I'm not so great at some things. They've taught me that being different is not just OK, but it's also something to shout about and celebrate.

'So here are *my* three golden rules. Number one: feeling my emotions and being able to channel them into the roles I play is a good thing. Two: whether I'm on the stage or not, I want to be authentic and real. And number three: even though it might be a bit more difficult for me, I can find my way with practice, passion and perseverance. Thank you!'

Everyone clapped, though the Dreamers were loudest of all.

Now it was question time.

Theo put his hand up first. 'Dyslexia seems a bit like dyspraxia. It's so confusing. All these labels.'

I nodded. 'Labels can be confusing. But, even without a doctor giving us a label, we use them anyway – things like "clumsy" or "weird" or "lazy". My label of dyspraxia makes me feel that my differences are acknowledged and celebrated, but they don't have to define me. I call myself dyspraxic, others might call themselves "person with dyspraxia", and many people will choose not to share that they have received a dyspraxia diagnosis with you at all.' I paused, thinking hard. 'And I think labels can be super useful for helping people understand themselves.'

'Excellent answer,' Miss Williams said.

More and more questions were asked, and I was able to answer all of them. I knew a lot more about dyspraxia than I thought! Eventually, my time was up, and everyone gave me a big clap and a cheer.

I breathed a sigh of relief. I had enjoyed that, but it had definitely been exhausting! Who would have thought that standing up and being yourself for ten minutes would be as tiring as three laps round a football pitch, and possibly more nerve-racking than performing in front of hundreds of people!

31

Party Time

12 May

Dear Journal,

Happy almost-birthday to me! For someone
who wasn't looking for much - only fame and
fortune - I've learned a lot on this journey
that I wasn't expecting. I used to wish my
superpower was like Dorothy in The Wizard of
Oz, and that clicking my heels could get me
anywhere I wanted, but I don't want that any

more. Now I finally get what Not-Granny meant – the journey matters more than the ~~destninasion~~ destination. The other day I was at Steph's and we watched a nature programme. Did you know butterflies have four stages to their life cycle? They start out as a very plain-looking egg, then a caterpillar hatches from the egg, and then a kind of skin forms round the caterpillar for the third stage, which is called a ~~cryst~~ chrysalis. I think this part is utterly amazing – the caterpillar's body parts and organs start to change through a process called metamorphosis, which is Greek for 'transformation'. It might turn into a butterfly after a couple of days or it can take as long as a year! I like to think we can all have a metamorphosis, except the most brilliant changes aren't on the outside, they're what happens inside. So even if we do sometimes feel a bit like a plain egg, it's good to know we are still on the road to becoming butterflies.

In other news, dear diary, I was at Effie's birthday party last night. It was awesome! We played pin the tail on the unicorn and musical chairs! It was a lot of fun, but now I need my beauty sleep so I can get ready for my own party … which is ~~tommorow~~ tomorrow!! Happy birthday to ME!

Love and drama,

Charligh G xxx

The whole of downstairs was set up like an Alice-in-Wonderland-inspired Mad Hatter's tea party. There were pictures of me in colourful paper frames on the walls, on the fridge and hanging from string on pegs. Me as a baby, me as a toddler, me the dancer, me the singer, me on the pitch – all the different Charlighs were on display, and I loved it.

There was a luminous yellow tablecloth on the table, which was heaped with afternoon-tea treats. Gooey cakes, delicate pastries and buttery croissants, and mini sandwiches with cheese, tuna and chicken fillings, as well as warm scones, raspberry jam and thick clotted cream.

My mouth watered, but I resisted taking anything since it was only 11 a.m., and my friends weren't due to arrive until 1 p.m. It was torture! And we were going to the roller rink at Waves and Wheels afterwards, which, believe it or not, was my idea! (I'd decided that standing up on two feet was overrated anyway, so I couldn't wait to have fun spinning in circles there.) My parents had rented it out between 3 and 5 p.m., and this week the theme was eighties and nineties.

I was just about to go and get into the eighties-tastic outfit Dad and I had gone shopping for specially, when I heard the doorbell ring.

I peered through the keyhole and whispered loudly to Mum, who had appeared behind me. 'It's Nancy-from-across-the-road.'

She must have come to pick up Rory and Reuben. She'd offered to take them for the afternoon while I had my special birthday tea and outing.

Mum smiled. 'Well, open the door then.'

Nancy was holding a pet carrier in one hand and a cushioned basket with a big yellow bow on it in the other, which she passed over to me. I could hear soft purring coming from inside.

My eyes widened. 'Are we looking after Tab – I mean Gerry – again?'

'Why don't you look inside?' Nancy said, laughing.

I handed the carrier to Mum so she could help me open it. Mum lifted the flap ... and gently pulled out a tiny, perfect kitten!

'Happy birthday, Charligh,' Mum and Nancy said together.

OMG!! A kitten for ME!

Mum passed the little creature over to me, and I lowered us both to the ground. I didn't want to accidentally drop it! Then I sat down cross-legged with it in my lap, mesmerized by the kitty cuteness in front of me.

'He's one of the last of a litter that was rescued by someone from Bramrock Cats' and Dogs' Home, where I've been volunteering,' said Nancy. 'He was very weak when they were found.'

I looked up at Mum, who had the biggest smile on her face. 'Nancy told me about him last week, but I wanted to make sure he pulled through before I mentioned anything to you. He was the littlest of the litter, but he's very gentle, very playful – with heaps of personality. Just like someone else I know!'

Right then, I felt as if I couldn't wish for anything more as I cradled the kitten in my arms and watched him wave his paw at me, then twist this way and that way before purring softly again. And, just like that, I knew he was going to be part of my family and another amazing new chapter in my story. I felt so warm and happy, as if the sun was rising up inside me.

'Thank you so much,' I said.

'What are you going to call him?' Mum asked.

He was a grey tabby with white socks and huge green eyes, which were playful and serious at the same time. I placed him back in his basket, and something about the way he was doing somersaults and twists and spins told me he was a bit of a show-off.

'I think I'll call him Rum Tum Tugger ... Tugger for short,' I said, smiling.

After we'd said goodbye to Nancy and she'd taken the Tinies over to her house, I played with Tugger until he needed a nap. Then Mum reminded me it was time to get ready.

After I came out of the shower, I sprayed my hair with blue hair glitter, then changed into an electric-blue top and denim shorts, which I wore over leggings. Mum helped me comb my hair into a side ponytail. I'd just finished getting ready when the first guests started to arrive. It was Talia (early as always), then Steph and Naomie, followed by Layla, Allie and finally Jaz.

'And what time do you call this, Jaz?' joked Steph, pointing at the clock.

'I've spent all morning doing THIS with a curling wand,' said Jaz, touching her hair, which lay across her shoulders in big loose curls.

'It's great! It took forever to crimp mine,' said Layla. She was wearing a baby-pink jersey dress with white high-top trainers.

'I love it,' said Naomie, whose own hair was styled into a high ponytail with a colourful assortment of scrunchies.

I had made a very special request to all my guests. Mum and Dad got me some really amazing presents, including two vintage summer dresses, a family ticket to see *Mary Poppins* the musical next month, a set of flavoured lip-glosses, as well as a wireless karaoke microphone.

So I said what I wanted was for the Dreamers to give whatever they would have spent on a present for me to a charity of their choice. I got help from my mum to list my favourites – as a suggestion – and decided on Age UK, Dementia UK and Friends of the Earth.

I had to admit that Steph was on to something with the whole giving-to-charity idea. It did inject this lovely happy feeling into you, and I'd learned a name for it that I'd definitely be using in Scrabble with my dad: altruism. (Noun: disinterested and selfless concern for the well-being of others.)

So there was no present-opening, but everyone had brought a card with gorgeous, lovely words that I enjoyed reading. Our afternoon tea was absolutely delicious, and there was barely a crumb left of any of the cakes, crumpets and scones we'd devoured.

Then Dad appeared, carrying a tray of tiny glittery green, purple and blue ring doughnuts with stars on them, and in the middle was a jumbo doughnut cake with eleven candles! Everyone started singing 'Happy Birthday' and, after the third 'hip hip hooray', everyone grabbed a doughnut. Then it was time for me to blow out the candles on the cake-doughnut and make a wish.

I closed my eyes and blew hard.

'What did you wish for?' asked Allie.

'She's not allowed to say!' said Talia in a scandalized tone.

All of a sudden, there was a loud honking at the door, and we all rushed to the window ... and saw a huge PINK party limo parked right outside my house!

'Talk about travelling in style,' Layla laughed.

'No way! Mum, Dad!' I screamed. 'Is that for us?'

'Well, we were tired of driving you to and fro, Charligh, so you'll just have to put up with the limo for this one afternoon, I'm afraid. I hope you'll be OK with that?' Dad asked.

Everyone cheered and gathered up their things. We all followed Mum to the limo, where she'd said she was going to sit up front with the driver, so we'd have the back all to ourselves!

Then I noticed there was a tiny spark still glowing on one of the candles. I blew on it one more time and made my wish again.

I wished that the love and happiness I was surrounded with today would stay with me wherever I went and whatever I became.

Epilogue

'Bravo! Bravo!'

OK, I'll come back out now since you asked so nicely. I suppose you're wondering what exactly lies ahead for the *Charligh Green Show*. The truth is, I decided to put the brakes on the whole pursuit of Super Celebrity Star status thing. What you're famous *for* is far more important than just having your name splashed everywhere for the sake of it.

Now that the garden project is finished, the Dreamers don't visit Flora House quite as often. As I wasn't Not-Granny's pen pal any more,

I decided to be everyone's pen pal, so each month I send out a letter addressed to the Flora House residents. Dad says it's good practice for when I start up my own fan newsletter one day – but I think he's just glad to see me writing more!

I do still think of Not-Granny, but I've been feeling EXTREMELY happy whenever I do. How lucky I was to have had my very own Not-Granny and all the happy memories we created.

I know that this is the end, and by now you're extremely well acquainted with me – warts and all – but I'd still like to reintroduce myself, since there have been a few changes since the last time I did.

Cue dramatic pause.

Clears throat.

Deep stomach breath and . . .

My name is Charligh Emerald Gorley. I live with my favourite people, who are my mum and dad and my twin baby brothers. When I grow up, perhaps I'll be in the West End, or maybe I'll be a news reporter, a late-night TV show presenter or even a Hollywood star. But, whatever I do, most of all I want to be myself.

Love,

Charligh Emerald Gorley (aka Charligh Green)

P.S. I'm dyspraxic and I'm fabtastic.

Acknowledgements

Writing *Charligh Green vs the Spotlight*, a book about authenticity, self-acceptance and the celebration of difference, has been an absolute joy and a process of both personal and creative discovery.

There are a few different people and organizations I'd like to thank for their support of *Charligh Green* and the Dream Team series.

Thank you to the editorial team who worked with me on this second book at different stages of the manuscript: Sara Jafari, Naomi Colthurst and Sarah Connelly. You have all been brilliant, and I appreciate all the invaluable support each of you gave me in different ways, to develop my story into the book that it is now from the early skeletal draft.

Thank you also to my agent Sallyanne Sweeney for all your fantastic support and encouragement with this series.

Thanks also to Camilla Sucre for illustrating two beautiful covers for the Dream Team series and bringing another of my characters to life, and to Sophia Watts for the interior illustrations.

Thank you to Phoebe and Michelle for all the great work you do to promote the Dream Team.

I'm grateful to the Dyspraxia Foundation for being such a valuable resource on dyspraxia over the years, and for the help in obtaining additional insights on the dyspraxic representation in *Charligh Green vs the Spotlight*.

I also want to say thank you to all the early readers who supported the first title in the series, *Jaz Santos vs the World*, especially the authors Jacqueline Wilson, Aisha Bushby, Maria Kuzniar and Carlie Sorosiak, who provided blurbs. I entered the book world knowing very few published writers or industry connections but your endorsement of Jaz made the process of my words going out on to shelves so much less daunting.

It was Maya Angelou who said, 'I always felt, if I can get to a library, I'll be OK', and I share the same sentiment. I spent a considerable chunk of my formative years in them, which helped shape me into the reader, writer and lifelong learner that I am now. I am hugely thankful to all the wonderful librarians who have supported the Dream Team, as well as fantastic organizations including the National Literacy Trust and WriteMentor.

Thank you to my real-life Not-Granny for the inspiration, and my real grandmother, to whom this book is dedicated.

I also owe a massive thank you to the following:

Every author, reviewer, blogger who has
    supported the Dream Team.
Every teacher who shared it with their
    class.
Every single reader who bought a copy or
    borrowed one from the library.
All the booksellers who pointed someone in
    the direction of my book.

And anyone – stranger or friend – who sent me kind words about my debut.

There were times when finishing this second book felt like an impossible dream, but your support of the first gave me such encouragement to keep going. And just like Charligh, I got there in the end.

As with every book, so many people from my past and present contributed to the final version, in a variety of ways, and I have listed just a small number of them above. However, if you have been involved in supporting the Dream Team in any way, once again THANK YOU!

Have you read the first book in
The Dream Team series?

Priscilla Mante

JAZ SANTOS vs THE WORLD

'Exciting, original and heart-warming'
Jacqueline Wilson

Olá! I'm Jasmina Santos-Campbell (but you can call me Jaz). You've probably heard of me and my football team the Bramrock Stars before. No? Well, you will soon because we're almost famous!

Well, forming the Stars was my genius idea – you see, I need to prove to Mãe (that's my mum!) that I'm a football star, so she'll want to come back home.

The idea was the easy part, though. Now I've got a team of seven very different girls and we need to work together, to be taken seriously as footballers – and to show the world that girls CAN play football!

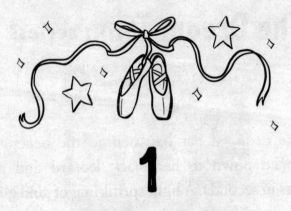

1

Dizzy Dancers

Every corner of Bramrock Primary dance studio was buzzing with excited dancers. It was the last class before we got into full rehearsal mode for the annual showcase. This year Ms Morgan's dance club were putting on a jazz-ballet version of *Alice in Wonderland* called *Spinning Alices*. We were going to perform the story of *Alice in Wonderland* through a series of specially choreographed dances.

I scanned the busy dance hall, searching for Charligh. The door swung open and in burst my best friend, looking so relaxed, as if we weren't already exactly seven minutes late for the warm-up. Her long burnt-orange hair was gathered loosely into what could only just pass as a dance-class-approved bun.

'Where have you been?' I said.

She dropped her bag behind the bench and stripped down to her black leotard and pink tights in seconds. A light sprinkling of gold glitter twinkled on the apples of her round, freckled cheeks.

'How about the stage diva sprinkles her glitter dust *after* dance class next time?' I said as we hurried over to join the others at the barre.

Charligh raised her left eyebrow in a perfect arch. 'Since when did Her Royal Lateness care about being on time for anything? You've made us late –' Charligh wiggled her fingers, pretending to tally it up – '*four hundred and forty-four* times this year alone.' Charligh's middle name was Drama. Well, not really, but it should have been. She exaggerated everything, although she was just about right in her calculation of my lateness record.

'Come on, girls! Last ones to get started again?' Ms Morgan swept through the hall, observing everyone's form and ensuring our outfits were just as she wanted.

We took up our positions at the barre. After all, we didn't want to be told more than once by Ms Morgan. She had a special saying about repeating instructions. It was 'twice, not so nice'.

I started my warm-up with a simple mix of pliés and demi-pliés. I looked at Charligh. 'This is our last chance to impress Ms Morgan before she decides on who is playing what in *Spinning Alices*,' I said.

'Either of you'll be lucky to even get in the chorus line,' Rosie Calderwood observed, butting in. 'Everyone knows I'm the best dancer and I'll get the lead role.' She flashed a dimpled smile that didn't reach her ice-blue eyes and smoothed her chocolate-brown hair that was already tucked neatly into a perfect bun.

Now, Ridiculous Rosie is *definitely* not part of my team. In fact, she's kind of a bad guy in this story, so any time she shows up you might want to boo, really loud. Rosie's the leader of the VIPs and, in case you can't tell, she is basically my arch-nemesis.

'Everyone knows Rosie will get the leading role,' Erica Waters gushed like a drippy tap. So Erica is pretty much Rosie's echo. She wasn't too bad until last year, when she was recruited into the VIPs along with Rosie's other sidekick, Summer Singh. Charligh and I call them the Very Irritating People. They had never actually told us what VIP stood for, so we could only assume, based on the evidence . . . I mean, the entire class knew exactly how many times Rosie had been to Orlando, Florida (three times), and just how much spending money she got for her family's annual shopping weekend to Paris (a thousand euros) and how big their villa in Spain was (very big).

Charligh tottered on one leg, stretching the other as high as she could. 'Rosie, do you take extra lessons on the side to become so good – or does it just come naturally to you?'

'Good at what?' Rosie said with her trademark smugness.

'Being incredibly annoying, of course,' Charligh replied.

I snorted.

'You cheeky little –' Rosie hissed.

She was cut short by Ms Morgan's three loud claps – her signal that warm-up was over. We gathered together on the mats in front of her.

'As you all know, this is our last rehearsal before Saturday, when we'll begin on all the group and solo routines for *Spinning Alices*.' She looked round at everyone. 'Consider this a final audition, because I still haven't made my decision on the lead solos. I have an idea, of course, but it's not too late to dazzle me today.'

I grinned at Charligh. I knew it! There was still time to show Ms Morgan that I could be lead soloist at this year's showcase. Mãe (you pronounce it like 'my', by the way, and it's Portuguese for 'mum') bought four tickets last year – one each for her, Dad and my brother Jordan, and the fourth for her youngest sister, my Aunty Bella. Mãe hadn't even made it to any of my parents' evenings for the last two years – Dad was so used to attending by himself now. But there she was at last year's showcase in the front row. It made me feel all sparkly inside when I took the final bow with everyone and heard her cheers above the crowd.

'OK, dancers! Split up into your groups of four. It's time for the mirror routine,' Ms Morgan said.

For the mirror routine, each person in the group took a different corner of the room and then performed an identical set of steps so that all four met in the middle. I was in a group with the K triplets from Year 5, so I sat down next to Katy, Keeley and Karina to wait our turn.

This year the showcase was going to be even more special. An army of butterflies took off in my stomach. My mother, who was the best dressmaker in all of Bramrock, was going to make the costumes. Imagine how proud she would be if I turned out to be the girl she had to measure for the grand solo dance at the end? I sat up, back straight, crossing my legs neatly, and noticed a plum-coloured bruise on my ankle. It must have been the vicious tackle Zach Bacon went in for today at lunchtime. *The next time I play him at football*, I thought, *I'll run rings round him.* I'd win the tackle, dribble fast and tight, flick the ball up and head it into the goal. Catching a look at my reflection in the mirrored wall, I realized I looked a bit silly because I'd been miming the actions. I quickly held my head and legs still before anyone saw. Too late.

Rosie waltzed over. 'You're such a weird loser, Jaz. What are you doing – throwing your head about like that? You're an awkward duckling who'll never grow into a graceful swan,' she sneered.

I'd been attending Ms Morgan's after-school dance club twice a week for two years now, learning ballet, jazz and modern dance, but I knew I could be a bit of an elephant among the more dainty dancers. I did goof around sometimes, but even when I tried my hardest, my grands jetés or straddle jumps never seemed to feel as easy to me as dribbling a football down the wing. Still, I wasn't going to let Ridiculous Rosie have the last word.

'Maybe the next time you go on one of your *amazing* holidays, your family can do us all a favour and just leave you there?'

Ms Morgan looked over. 'Jaz! I need you to stop distracting Rosie. We've all worked very hard to get our standards up this term. I won't let you spoil it for everyone.'

The rest of my group were standing in their positions, ready to do the drill. I folded my arms, stung by Ms Morgan's comments. It was dreadfully unfair of her not to notice that Rosie had started it – but then teachers never, ever noticed when Rosie did that sort of thing. Perhaps there was an invisible halo above her smug, heart-shaped face that made everyone treat her like an angel. As I twirled across the studio, I stared hard in the mirror to make sure there weren't invisible horns above my head, because I always got blamed for everything.

This year it *had* to be different. Mãe and Dad had been arguing a lot lately. And even when they weren't actually snapping at each other, there was this horrid feeling in the air that made me feel they were going to start. I had to stop getting into trouble so much because it was just one more thing for them to fight about – like the way they argued over the comments on my report card in Year 5, which were mostly 'must try harder', 'needs to pay more attention' and 'can be a bit disruptive'. So seeing me standing on the stage with a lead part in *Spinning Alices* wouldn't fix everything, but it would help. I could just picture it now: a star-shaped spotlight shining on me, Mãe and Dad crying tears of pride – and Rosie scowling from the shadows . . .

'Ouf!' gasped Katy. She'd collided with me as I began my second pirouette, crashing me out of my dream.

Ms Morgan paused the music. 'OK, let's try that again with the last group. Some of us –' she looked pointedly at me – 'are not paying attention. We need to get this right. How we make our entrance sets the tone for the entire performance. The plan is to make a dramatic entrance, not a comedic one.'

I ignored the snickers of Rosie and Erica from behind me and took a deep breath. *Focus*, I told myself. *Grand jeté. Plié. One, two, three. Pirouette, pirouette, pirou–*

BANG!

This time I skidded all the way past Katy and my elbow connected with the mirrored wall. Then it happened. It always appeared at the worst time. The Laugh was creeping up on me like a rising tidal wave. I tried to keep it down but the pressure was unbearable. It surged in my belly, pulsed up my chest and throat, and chugged out through my mouth and nose.

'Sorry, I'll just –' I spluttered.

Ms Morgan didn't let me finish. 'Take five minutes, Jaz. You can just sit over there and come back when you're ready to stop being silly,' she said. My cheeks burned as I saw a pleased smile flicker across Rosie's face now that I'd given her the chance to steal the spotlight. I watched her land gracefully on her feet after a series of three perfect pirouettes.

It was boring watching the others practise, so I decided to pretend I was actually on the bench, ready to run out on to the pitch to play for England in the finals of the next Women's World Cup. A sports commentator was announcing my arrival on the field . . .

Newly signed Jaz Santos-Campbell runs on to the pitch and immediately gets possession of the ball. She speeds down the centre . . . through three Italian defenders, passes neatly to Rachel Yankey on the wing, who takes it wide before sending it back in a perfect cross to Jaz . . . who SLAMS it in the back of the net with that great left foot in the final minute of play! What a pair of champions! Their supporters have hope again . . . it looks like they could win this . . . Wembley has never seen such an incredible final . . . !

The fans were chanting . . . *Jaz! Jaz! She's our star! Jaz! Jaz! . . .*

'Jaz! *Jasmina!*' Ms Morgan said loudly. I leaped to my feet, hoping she hadn't been shouting my name for too long. 'If you'd like to join us from whichever world you've drifted off to, you're more than welcome.'

Luckily we'd moved on from those pesky pirouettes and it was time to practise a new dance. It was a mix of jazz and ballet. Ms Morgan came over to my group, just as it was my turn. I took a deep breath, listening to the music as I moved to the upbeat jazz rhythm, and ended in an arabesque: front leg steady, back leg stretched out, and head tilted upwards. The best way for me to stay perfectly still was to imagine I had my size-five football balancing on my head. I held my breath while Ms Morgan's eyes focused on me.

'Excellent,' she said briskly, before she moved on. I exhaled and relaxed from my position. A seal of approval from Ms Morgan. Finally!

Later, as Charligh and I filed out at the end of class, Ms Morgan stopped me. 'Can I have a word, Jaz?'

'Text me tonight,' Charligh said in a stage whisper. I gave her a small nod as the others zipped out past me.

Perhaps Ms Morgan was feeling bad about how terribly unfair she had been to me earlier. Maybe she was going to apologize because she had finally realized – and not a minute too soon – that it was me, and not Rosie, who had the potential to be a star dancer. My toes tingled. I was already expecting Ms Morgan to give me the biggest hint that she was going to choose *me* as the lead dancer. I giggled, thinking of Rosie's face when I told her . . .

Ms Morgan sighed heavily. 'Jaz, do you still think this is funny?'

I frowned. Judging from the look on her face, maybe I'd got the wrong end of the stick after all and that lead role wasn't quite mine . . . yet.

Priscilla Mante is a writer from Glasgow, who is now based in England. She writes stories about brave girls with big dreams, and is the author of the Dream Team series.